MW00716429

ELEAZAR, Exodus to the West

Michel Tournier

ELEAZAR, Exodus to the West

(*Éléazar ou La Source et le Buisson*)

Translated and with
an introduction by
Jonathan F. Krell

University of Nebraska Press, Lincoln and London

Publication of this
translation was assisted
by a grant from the
French Ministry of
Culture – National
Center for the Book.
Originally published as
*Éléazar ou La Source et le
buisson* © Editions
Gallimard, 1996
Translation and preface
© 2002 by the
University of Nebraska
Press
All rights reserved
Manufactured in the
United States of
America ⊗
Library of Congress
Cataloging-in
Publication Data
Tournier, Michel.
[Eléazar ou la source et le
buisson. English]
Eleazar, exodus to the west
/ Michel Tournier ;
translated and with an
introduction by
Jonathan F. Krell.
p.   cm.
ISBN 0-8032-4440-1
(cloth : alk. paper)–
ISBN 0-8032-9445-X
(pbk. : alk. paper)
I. Krell, Jonathan F., 1952–
PQ2680.083 E5413
2002 843'.914–dc21
2001053463

For Coralie

Jonathan F. Krell   TRANSLATOR'S PREFACE

Reluctant Heroes

No historian can regard the biblical account of Moses and the Exodus as anything other than a pious piece of imaginative fiction, which has recast a remote tradition for the benefit of its own tendentious purposes.

Freud, *Moses and Monotheism*

The Bible has been a key intertext for Michel Tournier ever since he burst onto the French literary scene in 1967 with *Vendredi ou les limbes du Pacifique (Friday)*, a modern version of Defoe's classic *Robinson Crusoe*. One of the few objects that Crusoe is able to salvage from the shipwreck is a Bible, and it becomes his guide and comfort in the solitude of the island: "O Book of Books, how many hours of serenity do I not owe to you! To read the Bible is to be raised to a mountain peak from which I can encompass at a glance the whole island, and the immensity of waters surrounding it. With all pettiness swept away, my soul can spread its wings and soar, knowing only sublime and eternal things." [1]

The book of Genesis haunts his second novel, *Le Roi des Aulnes (The Ogre)*, unanimous winner of the prestigious Goncourt Prize in 1970. Abel Tiffauges, the protagonist, ponders the stories of

Adam and Eve and of Cain the farmer and Abel the shepherd, initiators of the eternal rivalry between sedentary and nomadic peoples. That rivalry culminated in the persecution of "Jews and gypsies, wanderers, sons of Abel, the brothers he felt so close to in heart and soul, . . . falling in thousands at Auschwitz beneath the blows of a Cain who was booted, helmeted, and scientifically organized." [2]

Tournier's fourth novel, *Gaspard, Melchior et Balthazar (The Four Wise Men)*, is a free interpretation of Matthew, the only Gospel that mentions the visit of the Three Magi to the infant Jesus. Tournier adds a fourth king, who misses Jesus in Bethlehem but in the end achieves a destiny infinitely more glorious than that of the other three.

These are but a few examples of the myriad biblical references in Tournier's seven principal novels and numerous short stories and essays. Variations on events surrounding the creation of man and the birth of Jesus are particularly abundant, and one critic has remarked that the Bible fascinates Tournier above all because it is a model for literary creation: "Visible or invisible, the Bible remains the reference, THE BOOK. Proposing the power of the word as the origin of the universe ('God said . . .') and founding every ambition to be, like God, a demiurge of the word, the Bible is without a doubt that which inspires and that which one must outgrow . . . by writing other texts, repeating, tirelessly, the Creation." [3]

Eleazar, Exodus to the West is inspired by another creation story: the making of the leader and hero Moses, as recounted in the books of Exodus, Numbers, and Deuteronomy. Moses is the model on which Eleazar shapes his life. Both are "hybrids" – Moses a Hebrew living in Egypt,[4] Eleazar a Protestant minister practicing in Catholic Ireland. Both are shepherds earlier in life

(Moses until about the age of eighty); both commit a justifiable murder to save a poor victim from a brutal master. Pestilence visits their two countries: Eleazar's Ireland of the 1840s is afflicted by the great famine and its attendant epidemics, as Moses' Egypt is struck by ten plagues. The dreadful forty-day voyage from Ireland to Virginia endured by Eleazar and his family is reminiscent of the forty days Moses spent fasting on Mount Sinai, when he received the Ten Commandments, and the forty years he wandered through the wilderness with his people. Snakes play a symbolic role in both lives: Eleazar's snakelike walking stick and his meeting with the Indian chief Brass Serpent recall the rod of Moses that metamorphoses into a serpent before Pharaoh (Exod. 8–12). Finally, as Moses was refused entrance into Canaan after the long Exodus from Egypt, so Eleazar will never set foot in California – after leading his family first across the Atlantic Ocean, then across the American frontier.

Moses and Eleazar alike are reluctant heroes of the type identified by Joseph Campbell in his *Hero with a Thousand Faces*. Here Campbell condenses the adventure of the mythological hero to a formula of "separation-initiation-return": "A hero ventures forth from the world of common day into a region of supernatural wonder: fabulous forces are there encountered and a decisive victory is won: the hero comes back from this mysterious adventure with the power to bestow boons on his fellow man."[5]

Often, however, the hero is tempted to refuse the call to adventure. Moses had fled his native Egypt after killing an Egyptian overseer who was beating a Hebrew. When God, speaking from the Burning Bush, orders him to return to Egypt to lead the Hebrews out of slavery, Moses balks, declaring that his people will not have faith in him. Thus God gives Moses the power to perform miracles: to turn his rod into a serpent; to turn the skin of his hand leprous, then healthy again; to turn water into blood (Exod. 4.3–9). Moses hesitates still. He will not be able to persuade his people to follow him, he laments, because he is "slow of speech, and of a slow tongue" (Exod. 4.10). Consequently, God appoints the eloquent priest Aaron, Moses' brother, to be his spokesman before the Hebrew people and Pharaoh; Moses finally accepts the call and agrees to cross the "threshold of adventure" (Campbell 245).

Eleazar, too, is reluctant to fulfill his heroic destiny. Persons and circumstances impel the timid boy to embark on the adventure he never wanted. Early in the story we learn that he had never desired to be a shepherd. It was his father who forced him to enter into the occupation that would eventually inspire him to become a minister, or shepherd of men (3). Like Moses, he is shy and often humiliated before his peers and his elders. He undertakes the great journey to America out of necessity, not choice, forced to emigrate because of a personal tragedy (he has murdered a man) and a national catastrophe (the potato famine).

Nevertheless, struck by the number forty, which seems to link him irrevocably to Moses, Eleazar is aware that he too has been chosen to undertake the fundamental, elemental journey that is the stuff of myth. Crossing the Atlantic, that wilderness of water, praying over the corpses of passengers who have died of cholera and typhus, "Eleazar knew now that the voyage he had undertaken would never cease to edify him and to clarify his faith. Is this not what is commonly called a rite of passage, in which each step brings a new revelation? Thus the dead of the ocean, whom he saw depart each dawn, gave him a profound comprehension of the shadowy beyond" (39). And in the wilderness of fire, the American desert, Eleazar believes that the snake who bites his son possesses "initiatory significance"; Benjamin's wound is "the price they had to pay to enter this sanctuary of aridity" (57). Water and fire: in the end, the lives of the two reluctant heroes are irremediably bound to these two primordial and opposite elements.

Tournier contemplates the two substances in *The Mirror of Ideas*. Science tells us that life began in water, "[y]et the flame fascinates us because it reveals the presence of a soul. Life comes from water, but fire is life itself, because of its heat, its light, and also its fragility. The will-o'-the-wisp performing its frail and ephemeral dance above the black waters of the swamp seems to be the poignant message of a living soul." [6]

Water has thus traditionally been considered the maternal and material principle, fire the paternal and spiritual. Gaston Bachelard, Tournier's philosophy professor at the Sorbonne, conducts a profound analysis of the two in *L'Eau et les rêves (Water and Dreams)* and *La Psychanalyse du feu (The Psychoanalysis of Fire)*. He writes that "next to the virility of fire, the femininity of water is irremediable." [7] The running water of streams and brooks evokes for the mythological and literary imagination both the sexual ("feminine nudity," *L'Eau et les rêves*, 49) and the maternal ("the milk of the mother of mothers," 170). Fire is "the principle of life"; [8] moreover, it symbolizes purity (*La Psychanalyse du feu*, 163–75), and, in its ideal manifestation, light, fire is "the basis of spiritual illumination" (174).

Later in *The Mirror of Ideas*, in an essay entitled "The Spring and the Bush," [9] Tournier remarks that from the time God appears to Moses (whose name means "saved from the waters") in the Burning Bush, the prophet is constantly torn between water, which represents secular, human life, along with the hope of peace in a "promised land flowing with milk and honey," and fire, which symbolizes the sacred, along with God's country, the desert (118).

Eleazar must make a similar choice, which initially presents itself as the dichotomy between his Protestant religion's affinity for the fire of the Old Testament and his wife's Catholic attraction to the waters of the New Testament. Eleazar comprehends this opposition as he ponders the faces of the chief protagonists of the two testaments: Moses with his "harsh, radiant mask," and Jesus, his face "clouded and wet with tears" (8). He will then interpret water and fire in geographic terms, as he struggles to leave green, lush, but corrupt Ireland, which "had stretched a curtain before his eyes, a veil of rain, fog, and chlorophyll that had masked the truth," in order to find spiritual enlightenment in the fiery desert of America, where "the perfectly dry and transparent desert air respected the brutal facts of biblical law" (66). The stark purity of this wasteland will face the challenge of another watery place, California, the bounteous Promised Land flowing with milk and honey.[10]

The Irish hero of Tournier's biblical western thus inherits the fundamental dilemma of Moses. It is not by chance that his name is Eleazar. Eleazar was the name of Moses' nephew: Aaron's third son and successor. Eleazar's two older brothers had perished in a sacrificial fire because they had "offered strange fire before the Lord, which he commanded them not. And there went out fire from the Lord, and devoured them" (Lev. 10.1–2).[11] This brutal destruction by fire lends support to Freud's assertion that Yahweh was originally a volcano god, "an uncanny, bloodthirsty demon who went about by night and shunned the light of day" (*Moses and Monotheism*, 273).

The honor of carrying out the priestly duties of Aaron thus falls to Eleazar, who is present with Moses at his father's death: "And the Lord spake unto Moses and Aaron in mount Hor, by the coast of the land of Edom, saying, Aaron shall be gathered unto his people: for he shall not enter into the land which I have given unto the children of Israel, because ye rebelled against my word at the water of Meribah. Take Aaron and Eleazar his son, and bring them up unto mount Hor: And strip Aaron of his garments, and put them upon Eleazar his son: and Aaron shall be gathered unto his people, and shall die there" (Num. 20.23–26; quoted and analyzed in Zeligs, *Moses*, 287–93). Eleazar, whose name means "Help of God," is thus the beneficiary of Yahweh's fierce justice, becoming Aaron's successor only after the mysterious fiery death of his brothers. Indeed, his name is shrouded in death: some folktales recount that he murdered his father so he could usurp his place (Zeligs, *Moses*, 292).

Eleazar the priest and Joshua the military leader inherit the roles of Aaron and Moses, respectively, and lead the Hebrews into Canaan. Tournier's Eleazar is an heir in his own right, the modern successor to two seemingly disparate myths: the glorious biblical adventure of the Exodus and the nineteenth-century myth of the American frontier, *le Far West*, which holds a particular fascination for the French as for Europeans in general.

Tournier roots his novel in myth, not in history. For he is aware that the two genres are essentially incompatible, as Joseph Campbell reveals: "Wherever the poetry of myth is interpreted as biography, history, or science, it is killed. The living images become only remote facts of a distant time or sky. Furthermore, it is never difficult to demonstrate that as science and history mythology is absurd. When a civilization begins to reinterpret its mythology in this way, the life goes out of it, temples become museums, and the link between the two perspectives is dissolved. Such a blight has certainly descended on the Bible and on a great part of the Christian cult" (*Hero with a Thousand Faces* 249).

This "blight" is illustrated by the lines from Freud quoted in the epigraph that opens this preface. Fortunately, Tournier is not a historian. Although history, with its dates and places, is present in these pages, it is but the skeleton of *Eleazar*. The interest of this novel does not lie in its illustration of factual events like the Irish famine or the struggles of emigrants settling the American West. Indeed, the simple events of the novel are clearly secondary to the symbolic impact of passages dealing with the Irish harp, the life of Moses, the initiatory journeys across ocean and desert, the conversations with Brass Serpent, and so on. Tournier's terse style – so different from that of his early novels – evokes the simplicity of mythical narrative and sets before us timeless issues and tantalizing questions from our mythological past: Moses' "dark, incomprehensible, even repulsive aspects" (22), his peculiar relationship with God, fundamental contradictions between the Old and New Testaments, and our own intimate bond with the eternal symbols of fire and water.

I would like to thank Michel Tournier for encouraging me to pursue this project, and Annelies Mondi and David Krell for their advice and close readings of the translation manuscript.

NOTES

1. Michel Tournier, *Friday*, trans. Norman Denny (Baltimore: Johns Hopkins University Press, 1997), 159.

2. Michel Tournier, *The Ogre*, trans. Barbara Bray (Baltimore: Johns Hopkins University Press, 1997), 357.

3. Françoise Merllié, *Michel Tournier* (Paris: Pierre Belfond, 1988), 250 (my translation).

4. See Sigmund Freud, *Moses and Monotheism*, 1939 (in Freud, *The Origins of Religion*, trans. James Strachey [London: Penguin, 1986]). Freud posits the thesis that Moses was not a Hebrew, but an Egyptian aristocrat.

5. Joseph Campbell, *The Hero with a Thousand Faces* (New York: MJF Books, 1949), 30.

6. Michel Tournier, *The Mirror of Ideas*, trans. Jonathan F. Krell (Lincoln: University of Nebraska Press, 1998), 51.

7. Gaston Bachelard, *L'Eau et les rêves: Essai sur l'imagination de la matière* (Paris: José Corti, 1942), 135–36.

8. Gaston Bachelard, *La Psychanalyse du feu* (Paris: Gallimard, 1949), 118.

9. This essay summarizes in a few pages the central thesis of *Éléazar*, whose original French title was *Éléazar, ou La Source et le Buisson* (Eleazar, or the Spring and the Bush).

10. Tournier's descriptions of California in *Eleazar* continue a Romantic tradition that viewed America as utopia. This notion was popularized by writers like Chateaubriand (*Atala*, 1802), and later by the Socialist philosophers Charles Fourier and Etienne Cabet (*Journey to Icaria*, 1842), who tried to realize their utopian dreams by founding communities in America.

For many modern French intellectuals, of course, America is more dystopia than utopia. Louis Marin, in his *Utopiques: Jeux d'espaces* (Paris: Minuit, 1973), chose to critique a very American – and Californian – utopia. His chapter is entitled "Dégénérescence utopique: Disneyland."

11. For a fascinating psychoanalytic commentary on this event and others in the life of Moses, see Dorothy F. Zeligs, *Moses: A Psychodynamic Study* (New York: Human Sciences Press, 1986), 204–10.

ELEAZAR, Exodus to the West

I

The young shepherd watched a great wave of soft, silver mist roll in over the ocean from the west. He knew that the afternoon would be dark and that no one would trouble his solitude. He was not afraid, but he felt himself sliding into a profound melancholy. Some time elapsed; then the faraway bell of the village of Athenry intoned its mournful and silvery music, muffled somewhat by the sea breeze.

Eleazar O'Braid understood the crude and halting language of the bells like his native tongue. What he was hearing was neither the angelus nor the carillon of a feast day. It was the knell, the funeral bell. He did not fear death. Only the adult, firmly rooted in the living earth, fears being torn from life by an unexpected and unjust death. The child and the old man float freely on the surface of existence and depart without suffering.

So who had died in Athenry? A short time later, Eleazar saw Sam Palgrave passing in the distance, standing on his cart, the one he had owned as long as Eleazar could remember. As he expected, it was hitched up to two black horses. Sam took good care of the four draft horses he owned because of the excellent revenue they provided. Two white horses, two black horses: for weddings and for funerals. He always used the same cart with side panels. But sometimes he decorated it with gray veils on which he hung the funeral wreaths, sometimes with white veils that entwined with the veil of the young bride in the wind.

The night fell like a new day dawning. The sea mist was alive with dark reflections and it sparkled with stars. It was time to go home. Eleazar whistled for his dogs, who were only too happy to hear the signal to round up the flock. It was a good hour's walk to Hezlett's farm, where he was employed. He noticed a tottering newborn lamb leaning against a ewe. Eleazar knew it would not be able to get back to the sheepfold by itself. He picked it up in his arms and held it close to his chest. Immediately the soft warmth of the animal and its powerful, comforting odor of suint enveloped him. Later, when he would think about the sources of his religious vocation, precisely this image would come to mind, these bright nights when he would carry home in his arms a lamb too weak to walk.

He had not wanted to be a shepherd, and, during his childhood, he had always dreamed of another occupation. In the village there was an old cabinetmaker with whom he spent many hours and whom he came to love like a father. He liked the forest odor of the pieces of wood that were drying in the false ceiling of the workshop. He had quickly learned to distinguish between the species of trees, some trivial, like the willow and alder that filled the marshes and lined the banks of streams; others noble, like oak and walnut, quite rare in Ireland; and, finally, some pieces of exotic wood left there by sailors who planned upon their return to get married in a bed of mahogany, rosewood, or cedar.

Eleazar was counting on becoming Charlton's apprentice, since he got along so well with him, when, to the young boy's dismay, the cabinetmaker suddenly died. Brokenhearted, Eleazar went to the workshop one last time and brought back as his only inheritance, a single shaving of a fir tree. For him this was no trivial souvenir. Tradition had it that boys who wished to become apprentices went to the big fair at Galway wearing on their caps the insignia of the trade they had chosen: a bit of wool for shepherds, a stalk of wheat for farmers, a wood shaving for carpenters, or a metal spring for blacksmiths.

So Eleazar plunged into the crowd one morning, but no one noticed the pine shaving sticking out of his hat and rolling back over his ear like a blond curl. When he met up with his father at the pub, he found him in the company of a local breeder who was looking for a shepherd. He was unable to hold back his tears when his father, shaking the hand of the stranger, committed him to a work he didn't want. Three days later, he left to meet the sheep of the Hezlett farm.

"What can you do, it's destiny!" his mother had said, folding his small bundle of clothes. "One must always accept one's destiny."

Yet it took many years for Eleazar to understand that she had spoken the truth, for the works and days of a shepherd obviously do not herald those of a shepherd of men. His brother, who had become a farmhand, never passed up an opportunity to treat him like a good-for-nothing and to ridicule his so-called work, which consisted of standing still in the middle of a flock. It seemed as though he meant to perpetuate the biblical tradition that sets the sedentary farmer Cain against the nomadic shepherd Abel and that forbids combining in the same fabric the vegetable product linen and the animal product wool.

And yet it was no small test to brave thunderstorms, hail-storms, and the gusty winds of autumn and to dash in all directions to bring together a flock scattered in panic. He had to over-come his repugnance and learn how to castrate the rams and brand the six-month-old lambs under the left ear with the styl-ized "H" of their owner. But his big job was the lambing, which heralded the end of winter as surely as the mauve patches of primroses on the moor. He had learned to help the ewes give birth and to dispose of the placenta. He knew that if twins were born one had to be sacrificed because no ewe has enough milk for two young. But above all, he had made himself a backpack out of sheepskin in which he would carry the lamb that was too weak to walk out to the flock, and nothing compared to the joy and pride he felt when he sensed against his neck the eager kiss of the avid and plaintive little head searching for a teat.

One evening, as he gathered his flock, he suddenly realized that a young ram was missing. Although there were about a hundred head, he didn't need to count them. The absence of even one was clear to his shepherd's eye, like a wound on a familiar face. He began to search the rocky cliffs, but the night was rapidly falling, and the flock, without its master, was in danger of wandering off into the moor. Finally he noticed the vague whiteness of a wooly shape on a rock far below. The animal had broken its leg and would have to be slaughtered. Nevertheless, he lifted it onto his shoulders and, with a mighty effort, climbed back up to the pasture.

Master Hezlett was gathering up the animals with the help of his dogs. Seeing that Eleazar had not returned, he had started out to look for the flock. The young shepherd saw at once the wag-oner's whip he wore around his neck. He placed the wounded ram on the ground, got up, and waited. Without a word, Hezlett raised the whip and began to hit the boy. He beat him for a long time: great whistling blows enveloped Eleazar from head to foot. When Hezlett finally stopped, Eleazar's face was barely human. A scar on his right cheek would always preserve the memory of this day: ordinarily it was almost invisible, but the least emotion would cause it to redden. And that was nothing compared to the open wound that lingered in his soul.

II

Sunday mornings, in the village church, the minister taught religion to the young people. Some barely listened, but others invested the holy story and the imagery with a deeply personal meaning. For Eleazar, it was the Old Testament stories and the New Testament parables filled with shepherds and sheep that were close to his heart. He identified with the good shepherd who abandons his flock to go out and look for the one lost sheep. It seemed quite natural to go from animals to men and to answer a religious vocation that his work as a shepherd had somehow foreshadowed.

He was seventeen when he became a boarder – thanks to donations from the small Protestant community of Galway – at the Gallican seminary in the town of Downpatrick, in Ulster. The austerity of the daily routine to which he and his classmates were constrained seemed wonderful to him, after the days and nights spent on the coastal moor with his flock. It is true that many of his classmates, young men of the city from bourgeois milieus, flaunted their superiority. For them it went without saying that Eleazar would behave in a rustic manner that they would have to excuse, since he originated from those half-wild lands peopled by backward Catholics. They made fun of him. Some held their noses when he walked by, pretending that he reeked of ram suint. They feigned surprise when he didn't go down the dormitory stairway backwards, since he had known only ladders at home. In the refectory, they laughed in disdain at his hearty appetite as he asked for more of the pureed corn that they ate every day, and that these refined boys found revolting.

He put up with their derision, amazed by everything he saw and learned, and by the unexpected privilege he had the impression he was benefiting from.

The church was decorated with a bas-relief depicting Saint Patrick crushing a tangle of serpents beneath his feet. It was certainly a great and holy mystery: no Irishman ever remembered seeing a snake in his country. They owed it to Patrick, the Apostle of Ireland, whose story, told by Jacobus de Voragine in his *Golden Legend*, everyone knew:

Saint Patrick on a day as he preached a sermon of the patience and sufferance of the passion of our Lord Jesus Christ to the king of the country, he leaned upon his crook or cross, and it happed by adventure that he set the end of the crook, or his staff, upon the king's foot, and pierced his foot with the pike, which was sharp beneath. The king had supposed that Saint Patrick had done it wittingly, for to move him the sooner to patience and to the faith of God, but when Saint Patrick perceived it he was much abashed, and by his prayers he healed the king. And furthermore he impetred and gat grace of our Lord that no venomous beast might live in all the country, and yet unto this day is no venomous beast in all Ireland.[1]

In Eleazar's mind, the reptile soon acquired the value of a mythical creature, heavy with symbolism. In the family attic there

1. Jacobus de Voragine, *The Golden Legend* (c. 1265; trans. William Caxton, 1483), ed. F. S. Ellis, 7 vols. (New York: AMS, 1973) 3:77–78.

was a walking stick, the shaft in the form of a snake, the handle shaped like the head of a boa. No one remembered where it came from. Eleazar came to view this object with a mixture of horror and fascination. Probably because he had been born and raised in a Catholic country, though from a Protestant family, Eleazar felt less affinity for the Old than for the New Testament – its miracles, parables, and above all the presence of Jesus. The serpents of Paradise and of Moses took him back to the dawn of man, to the prophets, to Yahweh, a world that seemed brutal and archaic to him. But his Lutheran teachers in Downpatrick disapproved of this view. They taught a return to the paleotestamentary source. For them the Bible was the fundamental book that contained all truth. The man of faith must never abandon it. He must always hold it open in his left hand and refer to it at random – even if there is no randomness for God – each time that a question, a doubt, a problem comes up. The answer could be found there.

Eleazar studied his lessons diligently, and he made an effort to penetrate their meaning. But he had a difficult time mastering them. In vain would the deep voice of the theology professor of Downpatrick ring out in the vaulted ceilings of the chapel as he raised his threatening and prophetic finger. Deep in his heart Eleazar heard incessantly the roar of the ocean wind on the coast where he had grown up, and the face of Jesus – clouded and wet with tears – conformed better to this country than the harsh, radiant mask of Moses.

He became aware of the important role of water in the New Testament: the baptismal waters of the Jordan River, the miraculous catch of fishes in the Sea of Galilee, the fountains and wells where women went laden with urns and jugs. And then there were these words that Jesus spoke to the Samaritan woman on the coping of Jacob's well: "Whosoever drinketh of this water shall thirst again: But whosoever drinketh of the water that I shall give him shall never thirst: but the water that I shall give him shall be in him a well of water springing up into everlasting life" (John 4.13–14).[2]

How Jesus would have felt at home in Connemara, where water seems to sing everywhere!

Above all, there was a spiritual value in the choice made by children responsible for fetching water. Indeed, when sent out with a bucket to get water for the family, Eleazar had always had the possibility of going to the pond a few yards from his house, but this water was polluted and had an acrid and fetid taste. On the other hand, the pure, clear spring that gurgled gently into a rocky basin was about a fifteen-minute walk away. His parents had never said a word about the quality – good or bad – of the water he brought back, but their silence weighed heavily on his conscience.

2. Bible quotations are from the following edition: The Holy Bible, Containing the Old and New Testaments in the Authorized King James Version. Guiding Light Edition, 1960.

III

At twenty, he returned to the moors of Connemara and, after spending a few days with his family, went to live with the Presbyterian minister of Galway, who had been willing to take him on as an acolyte.

The small Protestant anglophone community lived isolated in this aggressively Catholic city where everyone spoke Gaelic. The port had known better days, thanks to trade with France, Spain, and even the West Indies. But the seventeenth-century wars against Cromwell and William of Orange had ended its glory days. Some impressive vestiges remained, however, notably the Spanish Arch on which one could still make out this Spanish proverb: "En la lucha entre el agua y el fuego siempre es el fuego el que muere." [1]

Eleazar often pondered this mysterious sentence. Was it not an allusion to Ireland, land of water, and to Spain, land of fire, and did it not contain a pessimistic moral, if one considers that fire symbolizes enthusiasm, a young spirit, entrepreneurial zeal, and water the sad and discouraging constraints of everyday life? This

---

1. In the battle of water and fire, it is always the fire that dies.

phrase must have come from the lips of a Spaniard exiled to this remote northern land of mist and rain.

So was it a fact that Ireland was a land without fire? Surely not, but if Ireland had fire, it was one kindled in its image, a dark fire without flame, almost wet, providing heat, of course, but just a few bluish sparks for light, perhaps similar to the fire of Hell that destroys without giving light.

Such is the fire of peat, the only fuel of the great emerald isle. More than once, Eleazar had lost his way in the bogs where men, resembling statues of peat themselves, slowly cut out sods with long bladed spades. They placed them in loosely packed piles, so that the air would circulate through the clumps of peat all summer and they would be ready to burn by autumn.

This work was foreign to him because shepherds rarely venture out into the middle of these black bogs. But the deep and acrid odor had impregnated the air he breathed for so long that he could not distinguish it from the essence of his childhood. Would he ever be able to wash it from his body and his heart?

IV

He had met Esther during a dance that the landlords gave each year on the first Sunday after March 17, the feast of St. Patrick. Since this celebration coincided with the beginning of spring, the dance was a sort of matrimonial fair where young men and girls hoping to marry could meet. Of course, entrance to the dance was strictly controlled, in order to avoid any risk of misalliance. Only boys and girls assured of an inheritance of at least three hundred acres could take part. That would have been reason enough to exclude Eleazar. But as a minister he enjoyed a particular status, privileged from one point of view, but at the same time diminishing him in the eyes of eligible young ladies.

He dressed discreetly in his Sunday best, knotting a mauve necktie beneath his collar, and covering his heavy country boots with black gaiters. But most important, to give himself an air of confidence, he carried his "ebony boa," the heavy, exotic walking stick he had inherited from his ancestors. "It's the only snake in all of Ireland," they said in his family, alluding to the legend of St. Patrick. The austerity of his dress and the reticence of his manner made him nonetheless a kind of outside observer, determined to remain unnoticed.

Traditionally the dance took place at the little parish theater. On the backs of the seats, a floor was laid down; because it was level with the stage, it made a sufficiently spacious dance hall. On a dais musicians played the pipes, fiddle, flute, and bombard. Toward the end of the evening, to liven up the guests worn out by fatigue and alcohol, three players were called upon to perform on the bodhran, a goatskin tambourine which the musician strikes with a stick. The timeless beat of the drum united the crowd in a feeling of profound harmony, all the more precious and moving since for the most part they were families living on scattered and sparsely populated lands. It warmed their hearts to come together on this eve of the spring renewal.

The party was just about over and the crowd beginning to file out, when two young girls walked onto the stage. One of them held an Irish harp in her arms, a magnificently sculpted instrument fashioned from sycamore. Engraved on the neck were these simple words: *The Voice of the Spring.*

The other girl took a seat on an empty chair in the middle of the stage. She limped slightly and was leaning on a cane.

Many of the guests recognized the two young sisters – Juliet and Esther – of the Killeen family, related to the famous O'Malley clan. The oldest daughter – Grace – had married brilliantly two years earlier. Juliet lived in the full flower of her twenty-two years, anxiously awaiting a fiancé late in coming. The youngest, Esther, expected nothing and no one because her right leg had atrophied as a result of a childhood attack of polio. She had compensated for this infirmity and the loneliness that would be her destiny by developing an exceptional gift for music. No one in the county could match the purity of her voice, as she sang and accompanied herself on the Irish harp. Her sister helped her get settled in the chair and placed between her hands the instrument that has forever symbolized the Irish soul. It was in fact the voice of Ireland that everyone soon heard rising in the religious silence, when Esther warmed up with a succession of limpid and silvery chords. It was the song of the streams, springs, and fountains that give life to the Irish land.

Then the girl's voice, even more diaphanous, joined the song of the harp. She sang "The Last Rose of Summer" from the *Irish Melodies* of Thomas Moore, whose fame was still growing across the land.

Lost in the crowd, overcome with emotion, Eleazar listened to the liquid music joining girl and harp. Esther was not unknown to him. During the party, he had been introduced to the two Killeen sisters, and later, when a man had invited Juliet to dance a Scottish reel, he had remained alone with Esther, neither able to dance – she on account of her handicap, he because of the dignity of his station. They had exchanged only a few remarks above the din of the party, but each word of the girl was spoken with a smile that was like the dove that carried the olive branch to Noah, announcing the end of his trials.

He longed to see her again but had little hope of finding an excuse to enter the home of this Catholic landowner. One market day, however, a fresh and laughing voice called out to him. At first he did not recognize Juliet, whose dress and hairstyle had been quite different the evening of the dance. She walked with him for a moment among the displays of vegetables and the animal pens, and as they parted, she invited him to come visit the Killeen farm the following Sunday.

V

There was a large crowd on this beautiful day in May, when he timidly ventured onto the estate. Juliet made him feel even more uncomfortable by acting surprised to see him. She had undoubtedly forgotten about her invitation. She led him through the crowd to introduce him to her parents. With an icy stare, the father eyed this impoverished Protestant his daughter had dug up from who knows where. One never knew what Juliet would do next, and he was beginning to give up hope of marrying her off to an acceptable suitor. A penniless minister now! That's all we need!

Fortunately some new visitors arrived, and Eleazar could steal away. Juliet had disappeared, and he wandered alone among the tables and the greenhouses in search of the one for whom he had come. Juliet had probably said nothing of her invitation to her sister. But was Esther even there at the farm today? After two hours of fruitless wandering, he had started to edge toward the fence so he could slip away, when he discovered the girl sitting under an arbor. She was surrounded by young children, happily playing ball. The joyful surprise she showed upon seeing him made him feel better. He tried to join in the game, but the children, frightened by this stranger, fled, and he found himself alone with Esther.

She invited him to sit at her feet on a large cushion, and at a loss for words, they began to talk about children. Conventional wisdom claimed that they were all pure little angels fallen from heaven. The only duty of adults was to keep them from being sullied by the world. The way they were dressed, educated, and taught to play was based on this belief. Esther surprised Eleazar by ridiculing these traditional beliefs. Only someone who had little real contact with children could idealize them in this way. In truth, they were just as perverse as adults, although in a different way, in keeping with their age.

Eleazar was surprised by the lucid and freethinking nature of the girl. It seemed as if her handicap and her place as the youngest sibling had provided her with the distance necessary to observe her society objectively, without illusions.

They spoke of angels. Protestant theology is skeptical of these undefinable creatures that encourage – like the endless procession of saints – the unfortunate polytheistic inclinations of Catholics. Esther did not share this reticence. She delighted in the white and golden hierarchy of the Seraphim, the Cherubim, the Thrones, the Powers, the Archangels, and the Angels. The dogma of the guardian angel had troubled her as an adolescent, however. How could a girl not be embarrassed by the presence at her side, day and night, of this invisible young man who saw all?

Eleazar protested that an angel could not be called a young man without falling into an anthropomorphic fallacy. Certain medieval theologians had discussed the sex of angels. Vain discussions, for obviously, they are neither man nor woman, and they do not procreate. In this they are not unlike children, and mustn't one admit that only children, because of their weakness and their innocence, have the privilege of a guardian angel? That seems to be the meaning of this passage from the Gospel of St. Matthew: "Take heed that ye despise not one of these little ones; for I say unto you, That in heaven their angels do always behold the face of my Father which is in heaven" (18.10).

As he enters the impure age of adulthood, the adolescent bids adieu to his guardian angel, and deep down, he will never really get over this loss.

This idea that there was an affinity between the asexual nature of angels and the innocence of children clearly troubled Esther. The certainty that she would never be a mother created a painful void in her heart that she did her best to fill. She spoke of the cheerful, chubby little angels that people the ceilings of some Catholic churches, scandalizing the austere Protestants.

"An angel possesses both arms and wings: therein lies his power. It is an enormous privilege, because living creatures must necessarily choose between arms and wings. The bird, since he has wings, has no arms. Man has arms but no wings. It is not an insignificant alternative. It signifies a choice between involvement and contemplation, compromising oneself in the events of daily life or rising above things and beings."

"This same opposition exists in the political sphere," added Eleazar. "For the king reigns, but does not govern. He lets the prime minister dirty his hands in the everyday work of government."

"The angel, then," concluded Esther, "claims to unite the wing and the arm. Thus he fulfills his vocation of being a mediator between heaven and earth. He descends from heaven charged with a divine mission on earth, and he does his best, sometimes succeeding, sometimes not."

Sometimes not? Eleazar remembered in effect certain disastrous misadventures of angels gone astray among men. For example, who remembers the true cause of the universal Deluge? We always remember the good Noah in his ark, long-necked giraffes and lions with great manes poking their heads through the windows. But Yahweh's fury, and his decision to drown his creation in a vast flood, were provoked by the depraved lust of certain angels for the "daughters of men," and the resulting creation of a particularly terrifying race of giants.

And later, this destruction of the world by water was followed by fiery annihilation, for a similar reason. Two angels had accepted Lot's hospitality in Sodom, and the inhabitants of the city laid siege to the house to force Lot to hand over these handsome men so that they might take pleasure in them. "Even the men of Sodom, compassed the house round, both old and young" (Gen. 19.4), specifies the text, in horror.

The punishment of this lascivious city was a rain of fire that would sweep down and reduce it to ashes.

No, truly, when angels love humans it leads to no good!

When they said goodbye, Eleazar promised to write to Esther, if she would allow him to. She did.

VI

He wrote to her. Letters filled with biblical quotations and spiritual encouragement. It was his way of courting. She never answered. So, with the mad temerity that sometimes takes hold of shy people, he asked to meet with her parents. The fact that he was a minister guaranteed that they would consent to see him, but at the same time it totally concealed the purpose of his visit.

He arrived at the farm one Friday night, an hour early for the meeting. He had dressed up the best he could: a round wide-brimmed hat, a white shirt, gray floss-silk gloves, and his black gaiters. In the room that served as an office, the Killeens received him with a mixture of surprise and hostility, for they remembered his friendly relationship with Juliet. Could it be that he dared ask for her hand?

He bowed and blurted out his request all at once: Would Mr. and Mrs. Killeen accept to give him their daughter Esther in marriage?

Upon hearing this first name, Killeen gave a start. "You are confusing names," he said. "You mean Juliet." The situation was grotesque. Eleazar stammered: "I said Esther. It is Esther I am talking about."

The couple looked at each other. They exchanged a few words in Gaelic, as if they assumed that Eleazar, though born in this region, did not understand the language, or, more likely, as if in this language their words only concerned themselves and excluded the young man.

"It's our little lame girl he wants," said the mother. "We must give her to him."

"So be it," said Killeen. "But he mustn't have any illusions about a dowry."

Eleazar, of course, had not lost any of this exchange, and as always when he was moved by emotion, hurt, or humiliation, he felt the old scar burning on his blushing right cheek.

"Here, a younger sister does not normally marry before her older sister," said Killeen in English. "But we are above these kinds of formalities. We will ask Esther. If she consents, you will marry her."

The meeting was over. Eleazar said a few icily polite words, and then departed. When he left the farm, his right cheek continued to burn.

The marriage took place six months later in an intimacy that bordered on the clandestine. Because for this Catholic family, marrying off their daughter to a Protestant, a minister, no less, was to defy the entire society of County Galway. "They must be in a hurry to get rid of their cripple!" They never heard this insult, but they thought they could read it on all the faces they met.

VII

At first Eleazar believed he had simply married the woman he loved. He quickly realized that he had also married a Catholic. But perhaps these two aspects of his marriage were one and the same; perhaps he only loved Esther because of some nostalgic affinity for Catholicism. A Protestant minister of Irish blood. Surely these two aspects of his personality struggled deep in his heart and turned him into a hybrid man, a sort of religious half-breed.

Esther submitted silently to the rules of the community of which her marriage had made her a member. One day, touched by the docility with which she had abandoned the ceremonies and pomp of the Catholic church, he asked her if this renunciation was not excessively difficult for her. "Faith is an affair of the heart, not a display for others," she answered him. "And then, look, there is Ireland moist and green; for me it is the most beautiful and living of churches." And as if to illustrate her remark, she had placed the Irish harp between her knees and had plucked a stream of chords, fluid and pure, in truth the voice of the springs.

They had a first child the very next year, a boy they named Benjamin. Two years later little Coralie was born. They lived in modest contentment, surrounded by the small but affectionate Protestant community of Galway. One of the primordial virtues of children is that, through their education, they remind parents of the elementary principles of their culture. There are the first words spoken, then the alphabet, then history, geography, and especially religion. Thanks to Benjamin and Coralie, Eleazar felt he was relearning – with a mature and critical eye – what he had learned before about life and truth. The Holy Scriptures, which he insisted on teaching them himself, depicted more vividly than ever the great emblematic and founding fathers of his faith. Noah, Abraham, Isaac, Jacob, and Joseph constituted a familiar and grandiose circle that he visited each day and that inspired in him a fearful respect.

But it was the lofty and imposing figure of Moses who lived in him and about whom he speculated passionately. Moses speaking with the Burning Bush on Mount Horeb. Moses at first refusing but then accepting from God a terrifying mission, to free the Hebrews from the Egyptian yoke. Moses confronting Pharaoh, the Seven Plagues of Egypt, the great Exodus, the crossing of the Red Sea, the divine manna.

Yet what dark, incomprehensible, even repulsive aspects of this superhuman destiny! Why was it that this Hebrew child had to be raised by an Egyptian princess, which meant that he could not go back to his native people without betraying his adoptive family? Why was it that he had to kill the Egyptian overseer with a blow from his rod? Why did his brother Aaron, whom Yahweh had named second in command, take advantage of his absence – Moses had climbed Mount Sinai to bring back the Tablets of the

Law – to forge the Golden Calf? And above all, above all, why this incomprehensible and implacable refusal by Yahweh to let Moses enter at the head of his people into the Promised Land flowing with milk and honey?

Unceasingly, Eleazar ruminated on these questions, but when he mentioned them in the presence of Esther, she smiled and answered by quoting the Gospels. Jesus thus became the counterpart to Moses, the refutation of his terrible logic and the refuge from his frightening severity.

Esther liked especially to contrast Tabor and Sinai as the two summits between which the Christian revolution took place. When Moses climbed Mount Sinai, Yahweh refused to reveal his divine face to him, "for there shall no man see me, and live" (Exod. 33.20), he told him. He gave him the Tablets, which are signs cut into rock. Conversely, Jesus led his most cherished disciples to the summit of Mount Tabor in order to reveal himself to them in all his celestial glory. "And his face did shine as the sun" (Matt. 17.2), said the evangelist Matthew.

Thus the colorful imagery of the life of Jesus countered the abstract signs of the Mosaic Torah. And the Golden Calf itself – living insult to the Tablets of the Law – what was it but the child of the pastures and the milk of animal love? In truth, when Eleazar crossed the meadows swelled by rainwater, he saw more cows and calves than divine eagles and brass serpents.

Years passed. Benjamin grew in strength and wisdom. But his little sister Cora often betrayed – in a whispered voice and with lowered eyes – a disconcerting finesse and inventiveness. Her father, who hadn't paid much attention at first, began to listen to the sardonic thoughts she sometimes murmured as if to herself. Once, for example, after her father had quoted the famous pensée of Pascal: "If Cleopatra's nose had been shorter, the whole face of the world would have changed," she had mumbled a few words that he had sternly asked her to repeat in an intelligible voice. So, red with embarrassment, she cried: "Cleopatra's, too!" Another time, in his catechism class, after having discussed the Last Supper and the Eucharist, he had asked if there were any questions. Only Cora raised her hand. "The disciples drank the blood and ate the flesh of Jesus, but did Jesus himself drink his own blood and eat his own flesh?" Eleazar had been troubled by the impertinence of this question.

VIII

Then the tragedy occurred that Eleazar would henceforth call "the great tribulation." It was a fatal secret he shared with no one but an unknown child.

It was in the dark of winter. The oceanic tempest howled on the moor, tearing the clouds in the sky to shreds. Night was falling quickly, and Eleazar, leaning on his boa walking stick, was hurrying back to the house after a meeting with one of the village elders. There were several kilometers to cover in a checkerboard of small fields divided by dry-stone walls. He passed in front of a group of poor peasant houses whose thatched roofs were so dilapidated that grass was growing between the layers of moss. Since these hovels had neither windows nor chimneys, the smoke from the peat fire escaped through the always open door. Sometimes ageless, sexless beings were framed in the doorways, curious to see who was walking by, and a glance inside revealed the destitution of these people: a table and three wobbly chairs, a cauldron where the ubiquitous potatoes simmered, and, lying on the floor like some monstrous goddess of the house, a grunting sow surrounded by a cluster of children.

The poverty of the Catholic population, in which he had been immersed since childhood, had become more immediate since his marriage to Esther. He felt – as did all Anglicans – the silent hate that rose from this rural proletariat toward the English oppressor. The modest security he enjoyed, thanks to the pension he received from the government, cut him off from the poor people fed up with paying tithes to Britain. The Catholic priests – almost all from the poorest areas – lived off the voluntary contributions of the faithful. They understood the value of this material independence from a hated power and remained opposed – regardless of the cost to them – to any official aid.

At times Eleazar felt a surge of solidarity and affection for these estranged brothers, and, at these moments, he dreamed of converting to Catholicism. He couldn't help smiling at the thought of the enormous scandal such a decision would provoke in Galway County. For although there had been conversions in the opposite direction – Catholics joining the Protestant camp for motives obviously suspected of self-interest – the case of an Anglican minister joining the wretched Catholic masses had never occurred.

He had arrived at a desolate fallow field, bordered by the loose stones of the cliff, when he came upon a scene that suddenly brought him back to his youth. There was a flock of about a hundred sheep that seemed frozen in an anxious stupor. A teenager dressed in clogs and sheepskin stood motionless before a man who was giving him a brutal beating with a wagoner's whip. The boy swayed imperceptibly when the lash wrapped around his head. Eleazar ran toward them.

"Stop, for the love of God!" he cried.

He thought that the child turned his head toward him and was looking at him, but the strap whistled again and he closed his eyes. Eleazar felt his old scar awaken once again and bit his cheek until the blood flowed. His walking stick suddenly seemed to come to life; it rose toward heaven and crashed down full force on the man's head. The man turned slowly, stared at him for an instant, stupefied, then collapsed face down on the ground. Eleazar dropped his stick and knelt down next to the body. A thick white liquid oozed from the crushed skull. Eleazar raised his head toward the boy standing next to him.

"You shouldn't have done that," said the boy. "This is the landlord's steward."

As if the seriousness of the murder were proportional to the social class of the victim.

"We'll throw him off the cliff," he added. "Maybe they'll think it was an accident."

This "maybe" said much about the danger they would both face from this day forward.

Placing the dead man's feet under their arms, they dragged the body to the rocks. Then they threw him into the void where the rising tide howled from below. Eleazar was hurrying on his way when he heard the sound of galloping behind him. The shepherd came up to him. He handed him the boa walking stick, which Eleazar had forgotten. This instrument of the crime, still sticky with blood, would have most certainly led the county police to identify him.

From then on, he lived a nightmare. At each moment of the day and night he expected to be arrested. And if he was not in danger, was it not the young shepherd who would pay in his place? The decision to give himself up inexorably took form in his heart. He postponed it continually. He finally decided to do it no later than the feast of Saint Michael, at the Galway fair where the farmers renewed their contracts with the landlords.

He went to the fair convinced that he would sleep that night in jail, but he did not have the courage to bid farewell to his wife and children. He was walking among the noisy groups and the animal pens when he came upon a young boy who, with a pale smile, waved in a little sign of friendship before disappearing into the crowd. What was extraordinary was that Eleazar did not immediately recognize him. Quickly, he retraced his steps to look for him. It was the shepherd of the moor, for whom he had killed! And he wore a reddish scar on his cheek just like Eleazar's. He took a few more steps before realizing the folly of his reaction. The young boy was free, and apparently everything was going well for him. That was the most important thing, and he had to content himself with this finding. But they must not be seen together.

He returned home in a state of relief that bordered on intoxi-cation. And it was with this feeling of drunken buoyancy that he made the decision to leave, to emigrate, to imitate the miserable horde of his countrymen who each year took the boat for the New World.

IX

It was in mid-October of the year 1845 that the first brown spots appeared on the potatoes harvested in August. Discovered in 1843 on the east coast of America, the *Phytophthora infestans* fungus had thus taken two years to cross the Atlantic and infect France, Switzerland, Germany, and the south of Scandinavia. But nowhere was its devastation more catastrophic than in Ireland. The leaves, the stem, and then the tubers of the plant were successively attacked and destroyed.

It had rained constantly during that summer of 1845. At first the botanists thought this a sufficient explanation for the rotting. In truth, they were defenseless against this scourge that would cause a deadly famine in a populace that consumed nearly twelve pounds of potatoes per person per day. The moral authorities gave a religious explanation for the catastrophe: it was God punishing the people for their sins. They spoke of the drunkenness, the fights, and the rapes that accompanied every fair, every feast day, and every gathering.

Eleazar's opinion was close to this eschatological vision, but he felt that it was more a massive rejection of this accursed country.

His doubts regarding his faith – torn between Moses and Jesus, the Old Testament venerated by the Protestants and the Gospels in which the Catholics expected to find enlightenment – the humiliations he had suffered in marrying Esther, but especially the unbearable spectacle of the misery of the smallholding farmers, and the weight of the crime he had committed on the person of the agent of the Protestant landowner; all this accumulated bitterness justified in his eyes the final catastrophe of the potato blight and the emigration of thousands of Irish toward the Americas. When the earth curses man and heaves him up, he has nothing more to do than gather his most precious and lightest belongings and take to the road with his wife and children. Esther felt enough solidarity with the Catholic community that formed the bulk of the emigration to agree to the exile that her spouse desired. As for the children, they were excited by the idea of a journey they imagined extraordinary and adventurous.

Leaving was, in sum, easier than staying. It sufficed to yield to the tropism that led to the most dynamic and enterprising ports of departure. Landlords evicted more and more insolvent farmers. Entire estates were abandoned. Countless lonely old couples perished in hovels and ruined farms. The attraction of the New World was all the more powerful since the already sizable Irish colony in America – notably in Boston and elsewhere in New England – was freighting warships loaded with supplies to send back to their countrymen. These ships sailed back to America with thousands of emigrants on board.

Many Irish sailed first to England, leaving Europe from Liverpool. But others went directly down to the south coast and sailed from Cork. This was the way Eleazar chose. His departure had been facilitated by the surprising generosity of Esther's parents, who had lent him the sum necessary for the crossing – seven pounds per person, plus the price of food for the forty day journey. As Eleazar gave thanks for this munificence, Cora could be heard mumbling as if to herself: "They are only too happy to be rid of us."

But the little girl seemed to be living this great and mysterious journey as in a dream. When the family had begun to make the cruel choices of what they would bring along and what they would leave behind, she was the first to intervene in favor of the harp being among the objects taken. Esther thanked her with a grateful smile, and Eleazar did not dare object, in spite of the burden that this fragile and useless instrument would be. But was it not the soul of their dear Ireland that they would thus carry along with them?

For the rest, she was not interested in the preparations, and spent her time bent over pieces of paper, tracing the details of a big steamer fitted with sails. "It's our boat," was her only explanation, "it's my beautiful ship." And Cora drew the masts, the sails, and the yards with surprising accuracy, she who had never seen more than three mixed steamers in her short life.

X

When Eleazar arrived at Cork with wife, children, and luggage in tow, he knew that he wanted to cross the Atlantic. But he did not know if he would embark for Quebec, New York, Boston, or even Sydney, in Australia. In truth, he wasn't looking that far ahead. Everything depended on the immediate situation and on the ship that happened to be available. Suddenly things took a dramatic turn when news broke that an epidemic of typhus and cholera was decimating the departing passengers. They heard that during the crossings not a day went by when a body was not thrown overboard. Upon arriving in Canada, all the passengers were herded into the frightening squalor of the quarantine camp on Grosse-Ile. For the first time, Eleazar – who nevertheless had always lived with Bible in hand – thought about the plagues of Egypt that had preceded the flight of the Hebrews. After the fungus, the plague of the potatoes, now typhus and cholera were descending upon this accursed country. Was this not the sign that they should leave at once? But in which direction? Where were the Sinai and Canaan of this new Exodus? In the absence of any sign from heaven, one must rely on chance, but as the mystic Angelus Choiselus wrote, chance is God when he travels incognito.

Incredibly, it was through the voice of little Cora that Divine Providence spoke. The O'Braid family had already been wandering for two hours around the frenzied quays of the port. The haggard crowd of emigrants was constantly split, ploughed through, and scattered by carriages, wagons, herds of animals, loads being hoisted by cranes, and gangways and accommodation ladders that floated in the air before coming to rest on the ground.

Suddenly Cora stopped, and, pointing at a boat in dock, cried out: "My beautiful ship!" It was true. Nothing resembled more the drawing she had been laboring over for several days than the steamer whose giant form masked the sky. Three masts, two decks, a smoke stack as high as a column, and above all a predestined name: *Hope*.

Eleazar walked up the gangway alone and returned to his loved ones a half-hour later. The decision had been made, and with it the destiny of the four O'Braids conclusively sealed. The ship would set sail three days later for Portsmouth, Virginia, much farther south than most of the other boatloads of emigrants. The next day, they would start loading the five trunks that contained all their possessions. They would have to spend the following night on board because at dawn the ship would weigh anchor. They had been told to take along as much food as possible to supplement the skimpy rations, and also blankets, because at this time of year the nights would be cold. They knew nothing more about the conditions under which they would live for the six-week crossing. "Maybe it's best that way," Cora had said mysteriously.

The few hours they had left to live in Ireland were filled with so much bustle and bedlam that their anxiety and sorrow were anesthetized. Benjamin enjoyed everything and appeared to be living the happiest hours of his life. Coralie observed everything with careful attention and her brief comments were always surprising. Eleazar ruminated about ideas and questions that affected and sometimes upset his convictions. The lofty figure of Moses continually haunted him. It was during these hours of waiting in the middle of the throng of emigrants that he heard for the first time an obscure yet luminous word: *California*. He would not forget it. Although he was still young, he already belonged to that generation of emigrants who had to admit in all lucidity that they would never again see their native land, and that they must do their best to create a new one. This was a bitter truth, but it cured at once the unspoken anguish that had gripped his heart ever since his crime.

But for now, Esther required all his attention and all his help. Despite her infirmity, she worked tirelessly during these last hours, shopping for the items they would need on the ship, and making sure the trunks were prepared. They occupied two rooms in a sort of caravansary, noisy and picturesque, where men of all origins, morals, and classes rubbed shoulders. Eleazar constantly worried about the contact of his children with this crowd, which lacked neither adventurous rogues nor dangerously raving fanatics. "But are you yourself not a murderer on the run?" he said to himself, feeling his old scar redden.

Benjamin, dazzled by the novelty of this boisterous mob, seemed little receptive to the vice it contained, but how to know what was happening in the observant little head of Cora? One day, as the four of them were watching the colorful sea of passersby from the balcony of the inn, she had declared: "It's the throng of the saved and the damned rushing to the Last Judgment." Esther remembered that this was word for word the title of a painting in Saint Nicholas's church in Galway.

They had watched their trunks being lifted into the *Hope* by the capstan, but because her harp was so fragile, Esther had not wished to part with it and insisted on keeping it with her during the crossing.

Finally the evening of the boarding was at hand, and all four stood on the upper deck in the middle of indescribable chaos. The first mate struggled, shouting at the top of his voice, to keep this human herd moving as he wanted. A sudden push of the crowd split the family in two. They had to call out and search for one another in order to get back together. It was then they noticed that Cora had disappeared. Eleazar wasn't worried, thinking that she was with her mother. Esther thought she had stayed with her father and brother. There was a moment of panic. Eleazar began to question methodically any possible witnesses of her disappearance. Perhaps she had already gone down into the steerage, even though it was guarded and off-limits until curfew. They finally found a traveler who claimed to have seen a child run down the gangway and disappear into the crowd on the quay. Eleazar decided immediately that they would go looking for her, at the risk of missing the departure and losing the trunks.

It was then that they saw the little girl running along the quay toward the gangway. She jumped nimbly on. She was waving something that intrigued the people who saw her run by. It was the minister's boa walking stick. Eleazar realized that he had indeed forgotten it at the inn after having overseen the trunks being loaded onto a cart. He did not have the heart to scold Cora for this escapade. A somber and heavy memory had just welled up in his heart. Once already a child had run back to him with this cursed object he had left behind. He had just then killed a man.

Ship rules required that men and women be given separate quarters, the men in the lower deck toward the bow, the women in the stern. For Eleazar and his family this was a bitter surprise, for it meant that for the first time they would be separated – Benjamin accompanying his father, Cora taking her mother's hand. They would meet the next morning for the distribution of hot soup, and so it would be for forty days and forty nights.

Eleazar was struck by this number forty. For the first time, he had the revelation that his personal fate could help lift the curtain that so often made the Bible incomprehensible to him. In effect, opening the book to Deuteronomy, chapter 9, he read these words of Moses: "When I was gone up into the mount to receive the tables of stone, even the tables of the covenant which the Lord made with you, then I abode in the mount forty days and forty nights, I neither did eat bread nor drink water" (Deut. 9.9).

Was this not a sign, this crossing that would last the same number of days and nights, and could not Eleazar thus believe himself placed under the spiritual guidance of the prophet?

Even so, it was not a question of climbing a sacred mountain but, on the contrary, of sinking into disgusting filth. The lower deck reserved for the men in steerage class was a foul, cramped area. About a hundred privileged persons occupied the hammocks that swayed with the pitch and roll of the ship. But for the mass of the others there was just a narrow space measured out on the floor. The greatest difficulty was to walk in the half-light without stepping on sleepers hidden under blankets. You would walk on a hand, trip over a head, or step on a stomach, generating a storm of vociferations and insults. And the coming and going toward the hole of the latrine or the ladder leading to the deck did not stop. At times, arguments broke out, degenerating into brawls. Two sailors charged with surveillance would then separate the fighters with equitably distributed blows of their clubs. Eleazar did his best to keep Benjamin away from this misery, and he held on tightly to his boa walking stick.

They spent several hours a day together on the deck, weather permitting. Winter was coming to an end. The sky remained gray and wet, but they were spared the cold and, above all, the storms.

From the fourth day on, however, a ceremony that would be repeated almost daily unfolded at first light. The sailors laid out bodies wrapped in canvas onto stretchers: those who had died that night. A chaplain recited a few hasty prayers, and they were dropped on a runner in a gangway and into the green waves below.

It was Cora who discovered where the corpses were coming from. In the rear lower deck there was a ladder that led to a second and much larger lower deck, which stretched along the entire length of the hull. If the first two lower decks resembled purgatory, this second level was equivalent to hell. Lying there side by side on miserable cots were hundreds of sick people – some suffering from cholera, some from typhus, still others from illnesses sometimes diagnosed, sometimes not. Why agree – against all rules – to board these candidates for an imminent death? Because they paid the price of the crossing and because hopefully they would die en route. There is no such thing as a small profit. Esther could not keep Cora from going down with her into this place of agony to give what little care that was possible to the sick.

When they spoke about it to Eleazar and Benjamin, Esther and Cora both agreed to try to attenuate the abomination of those hours they spent attending the dying. Of the four, the minister visibly appeared to be the most affected by the trials of this horrible crossing. He felt as if he had undertaken a descent into Hell, and he regretted having forced his family to come with him. Of course, he was doing penance for his crime, but they had no blood on their hands, and their suffering was unjust.

But soon his mind, nourished on mythology and religion, made him see that the lower deck of the ship was an antechamber of death that was quite legitimate. He remembered in effect a phrase that Plutarch in his *Lives* attributes to Pompey, and that the Hanseatic cities had taken for their motto: "One does not need to live. One needs to navigate." From this he deduced the disquieting theory that a navigator is not wholly a living being, that for the time of the crossing he is floating in a limbo halfway between life and death. Do not the high seas have an obvious affinity with eternity? This being the case, if these dying people had bought their ticket, if they had wanted to board, it was obviously to ensure themselves a better prepared end, a death expected and thus more peaceful than the one they would have suffered on land.

This was revealed to him by words he heard in barely believable circumstances. He had volunteered one morning to say the service of the dead over three bodies that were going to be submerged. The first one had been taken care of with no problem. But while he pronounced the words of the Requiem: "Eternal rest grant unto him, O Lord, and let perpetual light shine upon his soul," he saw the sailcloth in which the second body had been wrapped move. He was going to signal, call for help, when the folds of the cloth opened. An emaciated, yet still young face appeared, and a finger touched his lips. He heard a feeble voice: "I beg you, for the love of God, be quiet, let me leave!" In effect, Eleazar said nothing, although more because of his astonishment than by his own will. The body disappeared in the gray waves, and Eleazar suffered the remorse of having been an accomplice to a suicide.

The days and nights were so similar in their horror that they seemed to repeat themselves indefinitely, so that the travelers no longer knew how long they had been gone, or the number of days left in their journey. Such was the ocean: a space where time does not exist.

Eleazar knew now that the voyage he had undertaken would never cease to edify him and to clarify his faith. Is this not what is commonly called a rite of passage, in which each step brings a new revelation? Thus the dead of the ocean, whom he saw depart each dawn, gave him a profound comprehension of the shadowy beyond.

On the plains of the afterlife, the souls of the dead do not endlessly abound and multiply, as one might think. No. Their number is certainly great, yet limited, and the cortege of the new dead who relentlessly pour in compensates for the progressive effacement of deceased souls who vanish into oblivion. For the dead live in the beyond only as long as there are living people on earth who think about them. The deceased are nourished by the memories of the living, and they disappear forever as soon as the last living person has devoted his last thought to them. In the underworld, souls radiate a life that is but the reflection of the thoughts of the living. A certain great man suddenly begins to blaze, his voice rings out like a brass trumpet or a bronze bell. It is because on earth a meditative assembly of people is celebrating his memory. Or, more humbly, there is a woman, a shadow of an old woman tinted by a timid reflection of color: at that moment a child has placed a flower on her grave.

The morning mist was rising slowly toward a pale sun when a green line appeared on the horizon. Immediately a cry rang out through the boat: Virginia! People thronged onto the decks. They waved their hats in a pathetic greeting as they began to distinguish the first houses of Portsmouth.

XI

When he reached the end of the gangway and took his first step onto the land of the New World, Eleazar was conscious of having accomplished a fundamental act. For an instant he considered kneeling down and kissing the earth, but he did not, thinking that the others would surely have thought it an excessive display. The land seemed unusually solid to these voyagers who had just endured forty days on the seas. In the limpid, cold sky, a harsh spring sun gave things a crystal clear outline. The Irishmen listened. They marveled at the pure, mineral silence that surrounded them. The chorus of springs, the whispering of the rain, the lapping of water in the reservoirs, the uninterrupted monologue of the fountains: from this day on, all these sounds, the soft, wet soul of Ireland, belonged to the past. And forgetting all they had suffered in their country, they suddenly felt homesick for the mists of the emerald isle. With a tender sadness, Esther held her sycamore harp, *The Voice of the Spring*, close to her heart.

To Eleazar's eyes, the New World possessed the simple and peremptory elements of youth and promised great revelations. The two children reacted very differently to the discovery of their new country. Benjamin, intoxicated with freedom after six weeks of imprisonment, ran from one curiosity to the next, like a giddy dog. Conversely, Cora plunged into endless reflections on the surprising discoveries she made. For example, she had been profoundly impressed by the black men and women she had noticed at the port. She had never seen black people, and, fascinated, she observed these skins, these faces, these trappings. She admired the complicated hairstyles, the small ears, and the happy contrast between their multicolored jewelry and clothes and their bodies sculpted from ebony. Esther was shocked by the indiscreet attention she paid to these people and reprimanded her with an annoyed look. Cora simply raised her head toward her and asked, "Why are there also white people in the New World?"

The question left Eleazar speechless. He had noticed, nevertheless, how black people were better suited to the Old Testament than to the Gospels. The people of the Old Testament, more brightly colored, more harshly contrasted, more simply human or divine – with their capricious and quick-tempered sovereign Yahweh – had an obvious affinity with the groups of blacks they watched arguing and gesticulating on the quays. And he noticed above all their laugh – full, resonant, solar – for in the Old Testament people often laugh, while it is but a pale smile that illumines the Gospels.

They had feared being detained and incarcerated in the port where they would disembark. Ominous rumors had spread about certain quarantine camps where arrivals from the Old World were made to wait interminably in unsanitary huts. This was not the case in Portsmouth, despite the stretchers that bore the survivors of the second hold. On the contrary, the port authorities seemed anxious to get rid of the emigrants as quickly as possible, facilitating their evacuation toward the interior of the country. The O'Braid family's luggage was loaded – without their being consulted – on enormous wagons pulled by six horses, and they began the long journey that would lead them to a tent village situated on the banks of the Ohio River.

Some days later, they arrived in a town called Cincinnati. It offered foreigners the spectacle of an immense pig farm and slaughterhouse, with all the grandeur and horror of Hell. Returning to camp, the visitors could still hear the incessant squealing of the animals being butchered and could still smell the acidic stench of urine on their clothes.

One week later the exodus started off again, now heading toward St. Louis. It was a big village, quite new, built in a few months' time at the confluence of the Missouri and the Mississippi, not far from the new frontier of the Far West. St. Louis was the hub for processing and trading tobacco, as well as the center for trade with the Indians of Missouri. The collective shipment of goods and luggage went no further, and the emigrants now had to make a crucial choice: remain there, on the banks of the two rivers, or leap into the unknown and attempt the crossing of the immense prairie and the mountains. Esther, exhausted and anxious, desired to stay put. Benjamin, only happy when he was traveling, insisted that they go on. Cora watched, listened, and did not say a word. Who could have guessed what the little girl was thinking?

XII

In truth, the decision was solely Eleazar's to make. It hinged on a word he had been hearing ever since his departure, without paying it much attention; a mysteriously beautiful word that circulated among the crowd of emigrants: *California*. It was in fact the name of a perfect country, thus named by the Spanish after a utopian novel situated on an imaginary island, California.

Eleazar, however, was not a man to let himself be seduced by a simple mirage. But shaken all the same by the marvels he was hearing about this California, he had recourse to his normal method: he opened his Bible at random to find the light of inspiration he was looking for. Now, luck – or Providence – had it that he fell upon these words from Exodus: "And I am come down to deliver them out of the hand of the Egyptians, and to bring them up out of that land unto a good land and a large, unto a land flowing with milk and honey; unto the place of the Canaanites" (Exod. 3.8).

He was immediately struck by the obvious similarity between the words *Canaan* and *California*. And when everyone around him spoke of this marvelous California, was it not as a vast, fertile land flowing with milk and honey?

Benjamin leaped for joy upon hearing his father announce their imminent departure. Esther lowered her head in resignation. Cora looked up, all eyes and all ears.

Now, the particulars of the journey were terrible in their simplicity. It was fifteen hundred miles from the banks of the Mississippi to the Sacramento River in California. First deserts, then forests, and finally the mountains. At twelve miles per day, that meant more than four months. But there was one absolute imperative: they had to reach the Sierra Nevada ("snowy mountain" in Spanish) by October. Any later, and it would become an impassable barrier of glaciers and crevasses. As the month of April had already begun, there was not a day to lose.

Feverishly, Eleazar began the preparations. He bought two covered wagons with four wheels and the chassis sufficiently high so as to be habitable. Metal hoops supported the thick, waterproof canvas, making the vehicle almost as comfortable as a tent. They piled in the trunks and furniture, placing the precious sycamore harp on a mattress of dried grass to absorb the shocks. Flour, sugar, dried and salted meat, rice, dried vegetables, green beans, broad beans, and chick peas made up their food provisions. One of the two wagons had a wood stove equipped with an oven for baking bread. But the heaviest part of the load consisted of sacks of oats for the horses because, according to the guides, they would cross vast stretches of desert.

These horses – four in number – were Eleazar's chief concern. The outcome of the journey, and perhaps even the lives of the voyagers, depended on them. Now, the market was crawling with unscrupulous horse dealers who tried to get high prices for wheezy old horses. He asked advice from the leader of the wagon train he had decided to join, for it was imprudent to venture alone in these vast regions infested with Indians and Mexican outlaws. The leader, named Macburton, had already crossed the continent twice. He then became a trail boss, paid to guide these motley crowds, often poorly prepared for the arduous test.

Macburton advised Eleazar to look for Cleveland bays, English draft horses raised in the north of Yorkshire. Their robustness and their calm and serious demeanor made them the best companions for the long journey across the continent, and since they were not very fast saddle horses, they were not coveted by robbers and Indians.

Eleazar did his best, accompanied by Benjamin, who was intent on having a say in the choice of the animals. They returned to camp, each holding by the bridle two horses matching Macburton's recommendations. Benjamin had insisted on purchasing a horse with such an odd coat that the seller was asking a modest price for him. He was white and speckled with red spots. He was called Gus, and people made fun of his clownish looks. He charmed Benjamin, who decided to adopt him as his own. The three other animals were a young bay colt called Buck; a gray mare dappled with black, which earned her the name Grizzly; and an impressive black work horse, warranting the name of Coaly, who must have come from the artillery.

At the last minute, the O'Braid family would gain a new member, and it was Cora who decided this. She had unwisely shared her bread with a lost dog who from then on had refused to part with her. As he had blue eyes, frequently a distinctive feature of huskies, Cora called him Blue, became attached to him, and begged her parents to adopt him. This was hardly reasonable, for all it meant was another mouth to feed. But when they asked Macburton, he affirmed that this breed could see in the dark thanks to its light eyes and was capable of feeding itself, hunting the small animals of the prairie at night. Eleazar gave in.

XIII

The departure was fixed for dawn, in two days. When the O'Braids arrived at the meeting point, they were struck by the spectacle that awaited them. More than forty wagons, together with horses, mules, and oxen, composed a scene of total bedlam. Men rushed around securing the last pieces of luggage and checking the harnesses. Two blacksmiths circulated with an anvil and a bucket of embers, shoeing the animals who needed it. The variety of people and vehicles staggered the imagination. There were enormous Conestoga wagons, resembling moving houses with their four wheels and six horses, but there were also simple carts with handles, pulled and pushed by young couples. One of the wagons belonging to the company that organized the train carried nothing but barrels piled one upon another. It was water, clean drinking water that would be sold to the settlers at the price of gold when the caravan would enter into arid regions. One mysterious wagon, always closed, belonged to a Chinese family and greatly excited the curiosity of the children. But no one could give them any information about it, and the Chinese themselves put them off with enigmatic smiles.

But the strangest, and often the least reassuring, travelers merely walked, a simple bag thrown over their shoulders; they could be the most adventurous, the poorest, or, conversely, the richest of the party.

Macburton's militia – a dozen heavily armed men recognizable by a red armband – were charged with supervising and protecting this little nomadic community. O'Braid expected a departure speech of encouragement, or an enumeration of instructions, in short, something that would denote the presence of some authority.

But there was nothing of the sort. They had been standing around for two hours when they noticed that the crowd was dwindling. In fact, the caravan had begun moving and was spreading out over the trail to the West. O'Braid was to learn that it was on the trail, during the hours they were walking, that news was spread, and that instructions and orders were issued. Macburton and his men let themselves be passed by the whole caravan, so they could speak with everyone; then they galloped ahead to regain the lead. No stop was scheduled for the noon meal. They just ate while walking. A bugle would signal the halt as soon as night fell.

The excitement of the departure was augmented by the warm sun and the inviting countryside of this early spring. The two wagons of the O'Braids advanced one behind the other, the first driven by Esther, with Benjamin at her side, the second guided by the minister, accompanied by little Cora. To conserve the horses, they soon made a habit of getting out of the wagons and walking at the head of the teams. The two children, accompanied by the dog, enjoyed running on ahead. They were curious to observe all the people and vehicles in front, and came back to report their discoveries to their parents. Eleazar frowned. He did not like all these people and disapproved of his children associating with them. Esther insisted that they let the children be. The joyful and colorful throng warmed her heart, and she shared the children's taste for human contact.

This first day passed like a dream. As soon as the sun set, the militia's bugle sounded the general halt. The wagons were arranged in a circle and the animals unhitched. Free to roam about the inside of the corral, like species clustered together, forming groups of horses, mules, oxen, and donkeys. Tents and fires brought families together, each staying close to its own wagon. In the event of an emergency – attacks from Indians or outlaws – everyone would be protected in the corral behind the wagons.

The children had never stopped observing the Chinese vehicle, whose secret they longed to discover. Finally their wish was fulfilled: shutters slid open, signs were unhooked, and in no time flat, a shop appeared . . . a real shop, a well stocked grocery store. There were of course dried fruits, salted fish, smoked meat, and dried vegetables, but there was also tea, coffee, cocoa, and a gleaming green shelf filled with cakes and candies. The Chinese smiled, friendly and triumphant, attentive to the customers who poured in. Only those who were looking for alcohol left disappointed. The Chinese, with apologetic gestures, indicated that that was one item they did not carry.

Alcohol was not lacking among the travelers, however, for very quickly a roaring fire was kindled off to the side, tables and chairs appeared out of nowhere, and a trio playing accordion, guitar, and drum attracted a laughing and boisterous crowd. Late into the night, one could hear the strains of music and singing punctuated by shouts. When he looked over toward the musicians and dancers, Eleazar's face reflected no trace of kindliness. In his eyes, they represented the worst of society, the kind he had hoped to escape from once and for all en route to the Promised Land. By what curse did this plague resurface in the wagon train?

The second day, the sky and countryside were just as pleasant as the day before. Yet the intoxication of the departure seemed to have dissipated. The voyagers were more serious. They seemed to question the horizon as if it contained the secret of the future. Over the following days, the sky became cloudy. It must have stormed nearby because the wind suddenly picked up, strong and cold.

"It is a warning," commented Eleazar, "but I fear that these fools will not heed it."

Friday, a violent argument erupted between a lone voyager and a young couple traveling in a light cart pulled by a single horse. They accused him of stealing the fistful of dollars that constituted their entire fortune.

Immediately, Macburton designated an advisory jury of six men, including Eleazar. The defendant and the young couple were each appointed an advocate. The arguments were promptly given before the entire population of the caravan. There was not the least shred of evidence against the solitary man. But he had a red beard, a sullen look, and no friends in the group. A majority vote condemned him to death by hanging.

Eleazar was angered by this expeditious judgment and tried to speak out in defense of the man. He was told to be quiet. A few minutes later, the man with the red beard was dangling at the end of a rope. In spite of Esther's efforts, the children, fascinated, witnessed the execution. That evening, Eleazar vigorously denounced a system of justice that prefers killing an innocent man to acquitting a guilty one.

"Red Beard was not innocent," Cora said suddenly.

Her father looked at her, stunned.

"How do you know?" he asked her.

"I saw him commit the crime," she affirmed.

"And you said nothing?"

Cora looked at him with her bright eyes – her only response.

"This child will always amaze me!" murmured the minister.

The next day, he had a testy disagreement with Macburton over a point that in his eyes was very serious. It was Saturday. For Eleazar, it was clear that they would rest on Sunday. But that was not at all the intention of Macburton, for whom there was not a day to lose if they wanted to cross the Rockies before the first snowfall. Eleazar brandished his Bible and read in a solemn voice: "Six days thou shalt work, but on the seventh day thou shalt rest: in earing time and in harvest thou shalt rest" (Exod. 34.21).

Exasperated, Macburton called together his advisory council once again. The problem was discussed. One of them pointed out that walking did not constitute true work, and so traveling on Sunday was not sacrilegious. Macburton proposed to organize a religious service before the departure. Those who wanted to attend would agree to get up an hour earlier. An Anglican minister volunteered to conduct the service. Eleazar, with a heavy heart, had to give in. That night, for the first time, he revealed to his family his intention to leave the wagon train and take a different route.

Esther was appalled, but she knew that nothing would make him change his mind. Benjamin and Cora welcomed the news with mixed emotions. On the one hand, the thought of striking off alone in the barrenness of the prairie appealed to their taste for adventure. But, because they had run up and down the length of the caravan, they knew everyone and had made friends. It would be difficult to leave them forever. But it is true that their hearts had become accustomed to this vagabond life, and they knew how to keep themselves from becoming too attached to things and people.

Eleazar exposed his plan to a veteran who had made the journey several times. The man began by exclaiming that an isolated family with two wagons would undoubtedly be massacred, either by Indians or Mexican bandits. Eleazar answered that the hand of God was worth all the armed militias of the world. The veteran informed him then that, in a few days, the trail would divide. Macburton's caravan would take the north fork. Eleazar and his family could, if they persisted in their plan, take the south trail. It would lead to the Sierra Nevada, to a pass that one could cross till October.

"And how will we know we are on the right trail?" asked Esther. "There are no signs, are there?"

The veteran smiled indulgently, and the little family's blood ran cold as they listened to his response.

"No, Ma'am, there are no signposts, but there's something better. The trail is littered with smashed wagons, ox carcasses, and human graves – when they're not mummies dried up by the sun. You can't miss it. And if you want to know ahead of time where you are going, look up. You'll see little black crosses floating in the sky. These are vultures. They know the right trail, you can count on it. And they keep a very close watch on it!"

And he burst out laughing through his beard.

If Eleazar's determination had been shaken by the words of the veteran, it was on the contrary definitively strengthened by the halt at Fort Laramie. An important stopping point for all the settlers on the Oregon Trail, the town was a center for buying and selling horses and mules and trading furs and buffalo hides with the Indians. The colorful spectacle of this multiracial crowd captivated the children: the animals wandering around freely, the dazzling displays of merchandise. They especially delighted in the street entertainment: boxing matches, jugglers and tightrope walkers, and trained animals.

Eleazar saw quite a different scene. After the alcohol and gambling that had infested the men of the caravan, he was now accosted by outrageously made-up women, immodestly dressed and reeking of strong perfume. They dared invite him to follow them to their brothel.

He opened his Bible and read: "I saw a woman sit upon a scarlet coloured beast, full of names of blasphemy, having seven heads and ten horns. And the woman was arrayed in purple and scarlet colour, and decked with gold and precious stones and pearls, having a golden cup in her hand full of abominations and filthiness of her fornication: And upon her forehead was a name written, MYSTERY, BABYLON THE GREAT, THE MOTHER OF HARLOTS AND ABOMINATIONS OF THE EARTH" (Apoc. 17.3–5).

From then on there was no doubt they were in Babylon, and he hastened the departure of his family. The next day, after brief good-byes to Macburton and the few voyagers they had become acquainted with, the O'Braids continued their western journey with their two wagons, their four horses, and their blue-eyed dog. Benjamin couldn't resist walking ahead of the first wagon like a scout, even though his father kept calling him back. Cora, always silent and attentive, observed and recorded everything in her little head. She surprised her father that night, sitting by the fire, when she alluded to the painted and perfumed women, whose bizarre behavior she had noticed. The minister contented himself with replying that they were "bad creatures," in a tone of voice that cut short any further questions. Cora absorbed herself in the pensive contemplation of the dancing flames.

A few days later they arrived at the junction the veteran had told them about. Up to now, they would only have had to wait a few hours for the Macburton caravan they had left behind to catch up. Resolutely, Eleazar chose the south fork. His face and his look changed from that point on. He knew that from now on he was making his way alone and was assuming complete responsibility for his wife and children. His only assurance now was the sky above his head and the Bible in his left hand. He constantly thought of Moses leading the Hebrew people toward the Land of Canaan, guided by the voice of God in the clouds and the Tables of the Law on the earth.

Cora was the first to notice that the grass was becoming more and more scarce and scrawny. Soon it would be necessary to break open the sacks of oats to feed the horses.

XIV

Blue was barking furiously at a spot on the ground where, from a distance, no one could see anything in particular. Benjamin called him, but to no avail. The dog continued barking, turning around the same center, sometimes jumping quickly back. The children finally ran over to see what was happening.

Red like the sand, with light yellow spots, a snake was trying to strike the dog with its small, flat, broad head, which ended in a short, truncated face. It was not a living face, it was a mask hardened by death and pierced by two completely fixed eyes. At the other end of the reptile, his tail, covered by horny rattles, was trembling nervously, making a dry crackling sound.

Cora knelt down beside the dog.

"It's a snake," she said, "our first snake. We have truly entered the desert."

She had understood that the snake is not only the desert's natural inhabitant, it is also its totem, and, in a way, its animal incarnation. From the desert, the snake takes its nakedness, its dryness, its ferocious austerity, and its hate for all other life. Its body shares the fire of the desert day and the cold of the night.

Its triangular head, horrible and hieratically perfect, tight as a fist, was stretched out toward the children.

Cora saw all this, but like her brother she had no idea how dangerous the American rattlesnake was. Blue, on the contrary, appeared to know, and although he continued to bark, he maintained a respectful distance, always ready to jump back out of the way. As bad luck would have it, Benjamin found a short stick. He grabbed it and began teasing the snake, redoubling its anger and its rattling. A second later the boy threw down his stick, screaming, and showed Cora his right hand where, as yet, no trace of the bite was visible. They ran back to their parents.

By the end of the day, Benjamin appeared to be wearing a purplish glove, his hand swollen with blood-tinged serous fluid. He was cold and shivering, so Eleazar wrapped him in a blanket and held him close.

Eleazar was acutely aware that this aggression by the desert against his son had an initiatory significance. There was nothing accidental about the rattlesnake's bite. It was the price they had to pay to enter this sanctuary of aridity. And so the life of Benjamin was not really in danger. No, truly, the desert could not in all fairness demand the life of this child. When Yahweh orders Abraham to sacrifice Isaac, his only son, the one he loves, it is only a test – cruel, certainly, but harmless to the child. Isaac would live and have a vast posterity. Eleazar's conviction was profound: Benjamin would not die from the rattlesnake bite.

Esther, however, was distraught. Because she was more intimately Christian than the minister, she possessed a painful sense of sacrifice, and knew that God's decrees can be bloody.

XV

The desert is a void filled with veiled looks. Eleazar might have believed that they were utterly alone. Nevertheless, these two wagons had not escaped the dangerous region of Indians and outlaws, as the family would soon find out.

That morning, Cora found an arrow stuck in the side panel of the second wagon. No one had heard anything. It must have been shot from far away at the first light of dawn or perhaps during the night by an archer gifted with night vision like the dog Blue. Worried, Eleazar examined it. The point was made of a dark green, razor-sharp chip of obsidian. The shaft was a carefully polished hazel branch. The feathers were fine and white, probably the down of a young kite.

Eleazar reached toward the arrow, intending to pull it out of the panel. Cora hurried toward him.

"Stop, Papa! Don't touch it!"

Her father looked at her, surprised.

"It's a good arrow," added Cora, "it comes from the night sky."

She was going to add: "It will bring us good luck," but she understood in time that her father – who held superstition in horror – would not appreciate this premonition. He stared at his daughter, then shrugged his shoulders and walked over to the horses to hitch them up.

The day was long because of the heat and also because of the suffering of poor Benjamin, who moaned and trembled in the first wagon on a bed fashioned out of blankets. At night they stopped by the edge of a dried up river bed. Judging from the distance between the banks and by the depth of the bed, where a tiny stream trickled, the obstacle would have been formidable during the rainy season. As it was, the crossing would still require a strenuous effort by the horses. The minister decided that they would rest on the left bank and wait until the next day, when they were fresher and stronger, to cross to the other side.

He would bitterly regret his decision that night, upon hearing a dull roar coming from the river bed. The weather remained fair, but it sometimes happened that a storm, far away upstream, would cause a sudden dangerous surge in the river. Entire wagon trains, following the bed of a dried up river, had been swept away and annihilated this way.

Eleazar could not resist lighting a lantern and walking to the shore. The roar became deafening. He could comprehend nothing at first of the dark mass whose great swelling he discerned at the end of the valley. An apocalyptic vision, he thought, thousands of damned souls banished from Hell by the anger of God!

Then he could better distinguish a few silhouettes and heard grunting sounds among the clamor. Finally a giant mass walking slowly on the opposite shore passed in front of Eleazar without appearing to see him. It was a male bison, a monster measuring about six feet at the withers and weighing a ton, perhaps the leader of the herd, most of which galloped tumultuously at the bottom of the river. The O'Braids were fortunate that their two wagons were not in the path of this migrating flood. Luckily, the dried up river was there to channel the transhumance of the herd. Nevertheless, for the time being, it would be impassable.

The next day at dawn, the cavalcade was proceeding at the same rhythm. The whole family ventured down to the river bank and became absorbed in the vision of the animal torrent rushing through the river. They had pulled Benjamin out of his blankets so he too could have the privilege of witnessing the spectacle, but his condition seemed to have worsened, and he barely paid attention.

By noon, it appeared that the herd was beginning to diminish, but another surprise was reserved for the O'Braids at nightfall. They suddenly found themselves surrounded by Indians, who seemed to have appeared out of nowhere. "I was told that the bison and the Indian were inseparable, but the Indian seems as discreet in his movements as the bison is loud in his march," observed the minister.

They were dark-haired, muscular men, dressed in skins and wearing feathers on their heads. They examined the horses and wagons, exchanging comments that seemed to express disap-pointment and disdain. Finally they grew still and drew back to let through a tall and majestic man accompanied by four war-riors. His headdress was made of shells, and he was dressed in a chasuble the color of sand.

Eleazar and his family expected the worst. The minister gripped his only rifle, a ludicrous weapon against the dozens of Indians surrounding him. There was a long, ominous silence that could yet have ended in death. Then there was an imperceptible move-ment that caused all gazes to drop toward the ground. Cora had just appeared among the men. She stood in front of the Indian chief and pointed to the arrow still protruding from the wagon. The Indians exchanged a few words and approached the wagon. One of the warriors pulled out the arrow, examined it, and gave it to the chief. He studied it and turned toward Eleazar.

"Brass Serpent salutes you in his country," he said solemnly in English. "This arrow brings you under his protection. Two days ago our best hunter shot it toward the center of the moon. Our mother the moon sometimes sends back the arrow to our hunters. It is a great favor for the one who finds it. We bow before the little girl."

At these words the Indians raised one hand and gave a guttural cry. Coralie, blushing and confused, buried her face in her mother's dress.

"My son is gravely ill," Eleazar then said. "Yesterday he was bitten by a rattlesnake. We fear for his life."

"I want to see him," commanded the Indian chief.

Eleazar walked toward the first wagon and pulled out a heap of blankets where Benjamin appeared to be sleeping. He brought him to Brass Serpent. The Indian slid his left hand under the young boy's neck and gently lifted his head. He brushed his right hand over his face and held it against his closed eyes. Meanwhile he bent his own face, covered with green tattoos, over the blind face of Benjamin. Finally the child opened his eyes and moaned. He stared, uncomprehending, at the forbidding eyes of the Indian, which stared back at him. "Eyes that do not blink," thought Eleazar, "eyes without eyelids, serpent's eyes."

"He will get better," pronounced the Indian chief finally. "Give him an infusion made from herbs and keep him in the dark until tomorrow."

An hour later, the minister and Brass Serpent were sitting under a tent made of buffalo hide and talking next to a modest fire that tempered the chill of the night. Eleazar had told him about the snake bite and the suffering his son had endured.

"I come from an island where all the snakes were driven out by Patrick, our patron saint," he said. "Yesterday we saw our first snake in the sand and stones of the desert. Your name is Brass Serpent. Teach me your wisdom."

The Indian kept a long meditative silence. Then he began in a hushed voice:

"There are two kinds of snakes. They are either venomous or constrictors. If it is venomous, the snake kills with a kiss. If it is a constrictor, it kills with an embrace. The first is but a mouth, the second is but an arm. But it is always by a gesture of love that it kills."

"This is the sign of a very profound perversity," murmured Eleazar.

"Malignant inversion is his vocation," continued the Indian. "In the beginning, he shone in the sky, as the most perfect of the creatures of the Great Spirit. He was dazzling, like the prince of the children of God."

"He was the most beautiful of the angels, the Lucifer, the Bearer of Light," agreed the minister.

"His pride was his downfall. He believed himself to be the equal of the Great Spirit. The soldiers of God fell upon him. They ripped off his wings, his arms, his legs, and his genitals. They made him into a column of leather ending in a mask: the serpent. They threw him to the earth."

"He was the trunk-angel. For he fell into the branches of a

tree, an apple tree, and there, the Bearer of Light taught his shadowy wisdom to the first human couple, Adam and Eve," continued Eleazar.

"Yes, but consider his head," added the Indian, "perfect, fascinating, beyond all beauty and all ugliness. It is like the desert that you have discovered here, situated beyond all beauty and all ugliness in its perfection. The desert shows us the face of God become landscape, and the head of the snake is his animal symbol."

"Explain to me the magic of the snake's head," asked Eleazar.

"The snake's head is formed by loosely attached bones," began the Indian. "The jaws can easily be disjointed. The whole head is thus collapsible. To swallow an enormous prey, for example, it bursts into pieces, and the whole body of the snake becomes like a great living sock that folds over the prey."

"As for the eyes of the serpent . . . they frighten, of course, but they cure! Look at mine that saved your son. Did you notice that my eyelids never blink? It is because of this that they have called me Brass Serpent. But the truth is, I have no talent at all. However, like the snake, I have no eyelids. So you see that we cannot close our eyes, even in the sun."

"The eyelid – its closing, the warm and dark moisture with which it caresses the eye – it is the very organ of my country, mild and rainy Ireland," mused Eleazar.

"Eagles have eyelids. Lizards, turtles, and iguanas have eyelids. Only the snake has no eyelids."

"But it can be stated in other terms. One can also say that the snake is dressed in an immense eyelid, because its eyes are covered by the skin it sheds once a year. Where the eyes are, one can see that the skin is transparent. The snake is but a face, a look."

He was silent for a long time. Then he gestured toward his bare chest and thighs.

"I see you are wrapped up in clothes and furs from your feet to your head to shield yourself from the chill of the night," he said finally. "Only your face is bare, because only your face does not fear the cold. Look at me. I am naked from head to foot and I am not cold. Because everywhere I am face!"

Back with his family, contemplating the peaceful sleep of Benjamin, Eleazar knew that the child was better.

He opened his Bible and read:

And the Lord sent fiery serpents among the people, and they bit the people; and much people of Israel died. Therefore the people came to Moses, and said, We have sinned, for we have spoken against the Lord, and against thee; pray unto the Lord, that he take away the serpents from us. And Moses prayed for the people. And the Lord said unto Moses, Make thee a fiery serpent, and set it upon a pole: and it shall come to pass, that every one that is bitten, when he looketh upon it, shall live. And Moses made a serpent of brass, and put it upon a pole, and it came to pass, that if a serpent had bitten any man, when he beheld the serpent of brass, he lived. (Num. 21.6–9)

"Everywhere I am face," the Indian had said. This naked look, with the power to kill and to heal, is the very mystery of God, thought Eleazar.

The next morning, Benjamin seemed completely recuperated from his wound. His right hand looked normal again. But his face was marked by deep black circles under the eyes that had survived the burning, blinkless gaze of Brass Serpent.

A short time later, Esther was surprised to hear Cora explaining to her brother the lesson she had extracted from their meeting with the Indian chief.

"You understand, Benjamin, Lucifer means Bearer of Light. Lucifer wanted to bring light to Adam and Eve. But that light was too heavy for him. His arms were full of it. He tumbled down from the sky. He lost his arms and legs and fell into the branches of a tree. An apple tree. Even so, he gave his light to Adam and Eve, but it was a light all turned around, all backwards, a bad light . . ."

XVI

The last green saguaros and Joshua trees had disappeared over the horizon. In the glorious sun, the air shimmered on the pink sand of the plateau. Eleazar stopped before a withered thorn bush. He took off his hat to feel the full strength of the light, but also perhaps in a gesture of respect. He had a sudden revelation of the deep meaning of his journey. He understood now that his native land, and especially the sky of his childhood and youth, had stretched a curtain before his eyes, a veil of rain, fog, and chlorophyll that had masked the truth. Green Ireland had come between him and the Scriptures. Only the perfectly dry and transparent desert air respected the brutal facts of biblical law.

He lowered his eyes toward the thorn bush. He was not insane enough to expect it to burst into flames or a voice to rise out of it. He was not a madman who thought he was Moses. Nevertheless he felt his own story to be powerfully attracted to, modeled on, and lent significance by the radiance of the Prophet's destiny, as a pile of iron filings is given order and direction by a magnet's field. Moses' imposing adventure served as a key to decipher the mediocre events of his own life.

Thus his hybrid situation as a Protestant in a Catholic country was illuminated by Moses' equivocal status: a Hebrew child saved, taken in, and raised by an Egyptian princess. There was an undeniable affinity between the crime he had committed in killing the steward and Moses' murder of the Egyptian who was thrashing a Hebrew. The potato blight and the epidemics of typhus and cholera that had ravaged Ireland echoed the plagues of Egypt. The forty-day ordeal suffered on the *Hope* corresponded to the forty days that Moses fasted on Mount Sinai. And then there was Moses' staff, transformed several times into a serpent, reappearing in the ebony boa walking stick of the O'Braids, this serpent cast out of Ireland but waiting for Eleazar in the desert in the form of an Indian chief.

But it was especially the entrance into Canaan that took on a formidable meaning in Eleazar's eyes. For centuries, Yahweh's forbidding Moses to enter the Promised Land had scandalized generations of Jewish and Christian theologians. How could the finest son of Israel, the greatest of prophets, the only herald of the Torah in the drama of the Burning Bush and the Sinai, be treated like this by the divine master of all justice? [1]

Eleazar had scoffed at the traditional explanation for this disgrace, which seemed ludicrous. Twice Moses made water spring from a rock with Yahweh's help. The first time was at Raphidim. The Hebrews had revolted. "Wherefore is this that thou hast brought us up out of Egypt, to kill us and our children and our cattle with thirst? And Moses cried unto the Lord, saying, What shall I do unto this people? they be almost ready to stone me" (Exod. 17.3–4). So Yahweh gave him the power to make water spring from the rock at Horeb with a blow from his staff.

---

1. This question is borrowed verbatim from André Chouraqui's *Moïse* (Editions du Rocher, p. 204), the book that inspired this novel.

The second episode occurred a bit later at Meriba. "And wherefore have ye made us to come up out of Egypt, to bring us in unto this evil place?" cried the Hebrews. "It is no place of seed, or of figs, or of vines, or of pomegranates; neither is there any water to drink" (Num. 20.5). Once again Moses implored Yahweh, who again gave him the power to bring water from a rock with his staff. Moses lifted his hand and struck the rock twice, and water flowed from it abundantly.

It was this second blow to the rock that must have irritated Yahweh, who saw it as a lack of confidence, justifying his terrible decree: Moses would not enter the Promised Land.

Eleazar now knew that he had been wrong to scorn this justification of Moses' disgrace, because it contained the key to the ancient enigma. It was in effect a fundamental choice between the Spring and the Bush that Yahweh forced on his prophet.

Led by Moses, the Hebrews had triumphed over the obstinacy of the Egyptians. They crossed the Red Sea and after three months of wandering through the desert finally arrived at the foot of Mount Sinai. Yahweh welcomed them there with these words: "Ye have seen what I did unto the Egyptians, and how I bare you on eagles' wings, and brought you unto myself. Now therefore, if ye will obey my voice indeed, and keep my covenant, then ye shall be a peculiar treasure unto me above all people: for all the earth is mine. And ye shall be unto me a kingdom of priests, and an holy nation" (Exod. 19.4–6).

There was a huge misunderstanding here, for the Hebrews had no intention of becoming a people of anchorites permanently settled in the aridity of the desert. They had wives, children, and livestock. They wanted land to cultivate, and for that, water, water, and more water! Moses, who was constantly promising them the opposite of the desert, a land "flowing with milk and honey," knew this all too well. He was torn between Yahweh and the Hebrew people, between the Burning Bush and the Source of running water, and between the sacred and the profane.

The episode of the Golden Calf is the triumph of the profane: the Hebrew's instinctive and puerile search for milk and the nurturing cow. The wrath of Yahweh burns hotly. He proclaims that he will annihilate this people, this whining mass with their idiotic herds, these women burdened with bawling and peeing children. The lowly spring flows down toward the valley; the water's irresistible vocation is to descend, to be absorbed between the rocks, to disappear in the sands. Water extinguishes the Burning Bush.

But the Bush rises vertically and victoriously toward the sky. Yahweh wants to stay alone with Moses. "I will make of thee a great nation," he promises (Exod. 32.10).

Moses begs him to spare the Hebrews and to give them one last chance, and Yahweh acquiesces, but on Mount Nebo his will to remain alone with his prophet will triumph.

It is our own mediocrity that makes us see Yahweh's refusal to permit Moses to enter the Promised Land as a punishment. In truth it is an act of love. But Yahweh's love is jealous and tyrannical, and the chosen one can but welcome it with anguish and trembling.

Moses means "saved from the waters," and his life will be defined by his relationship to the liquid element, his life will be split between the Bush and the Spring. And his death will be the definitive triumph of the Bush over the Spring. On Mount Nebo, at the threshold of the Promised Land, he hears Yahweh repeat his promise to keep Moses close to Him in the country of the

Burning Bush. The Hebrew people, following the downward slope of the springs, will descend into the green valley under the leadership of Joshua. Moses will die "from the breath of Yahweh," says the Hebrew text (Deuteronomy 34.5), and some translators write "by order of Yahweh;" but others say "from Yahweh's kiss."

But since his meeting with Brass Serpent, Eleazar wondered if Yahweh hadn't killed Moses simply by revealing his face to him. Had he not told him on Sinai: "No, thou shalt not see my face, for a man who has seen the face of God cannot live."

Yahweh jealously carried away Moses' remains and forbade the Hebrews to look for them for fear they might worship him as a god (Deuteronomy 34.6).

This was Eleazar's revelation – inspired by the desert of the New World where he had ventured – concerning the fate of Moses.

When he returned to the camp, the two wagons and his family, he no longer looked with the same eyes at these beings and these things that had been his whole life.

XVII

The Red Hand (Mano Roja) had become sadly infamous for its numerous bold crimes: stagecoach robberies, bank holdups, cattle and horse thefts, wagon train raids, and so on. Its five members had a price on their heads that adorned posters tacked up in cities, settlements, and meeting points. So far they had evaded all organized efforts to capture them.

Very little was known about them, except that they came from northern Mexico, and that their names were Old Pedro, Lucky Felipe, Cunning Luis, One-Eyed Alejo, and Cruel José. This José was especially known for the cold determination with which he attacked and killed, although he was the youngest and smallest of the gang. Perhaps he felt a need to compensate for his youth by an extra dose of viciousness. His story could be summarized by a few dark events, quite common in this society. His father, a worker in a silver mine, had perished in a cave-in, leaving his mother with three children. He was the eldest and could not get along with his mother's second husband, who drank and beat his wife and children. After a last violent scene in which he left his stepfather for dead, José was forced to flee. He had then taken on any odd jobs he could, given his young age, his weak build, and the fact that he had to be constantly on the move to elude the police.

In truth, he thought constantly about his mother, his sisters, and the village priest who had taught him everything and had encouraged him to join the parish choir. Sometimes, when he was alone, he would hum the melody of a simple hymn, until a strange lump would rise up in his throat. Then he would curse himself and furiously kick the stones lying on the path.

He was about penniless when one day he witnessed a robber being chased by a band of villagers. By chance, he was able to lead the pursuers off on a false trail and thus save the robber. A few days later, supported by One-Eyed Alejo, who owed him his life, he was admitted to the Red Hand. He commanded respect because he knew how to read, did not drink, and was an uncannily good shot, but his companions did not really like him. To them he seemed to belong to another species. His youth and his frailty contrasted in a troubling manner with the wisdom of the opinions he gave before each operation. The truth was that his companions were a little afraid of him. It was he who had suggested to the gang to move off to the north in the direction of these vast spaces crisscrossed by emigrants and cattle herds. So the Red Hand had been wandering in the prairie for a month and was beginning to despair of ever finding a profitable target, when Lucky Felipe had spotted the O'Braid family.

Concealed behind a rock, he had seen them pass close by. "A man, a woman, and two children," he had reported to his partners. "Plus a dog, who could be real trouble. He almost got me caught. We'll have to start by getting rid of that dirty mutt."

The job did not seem to present any major difficulties. Pedro rubbed his hands. Finally a juicy hit after such a long wait! Felipe calculated what the four horses, the two wagons, and their load – perhaps valuable – would bring on the market. Alejo's single eye sparkled with cruel joy. Not one of these desperados seemed to think about the four bodies they would leave to the vultures and coyotes of the desert.

One evening, José volunteered to get closer to the O'Braids under cover of darkness, to better scrutinize them and measure their ability to defend themselves. No one objected.

He penetrated into the shadows and was very quickly able to orient himself thanks to the point of light formed by the voyagers' campfire. He was surprised by the feeling of exasperated anger he felt at such negligence and imprudence. How could the head of a family expose his wife, children, and himself like this to the dangers of the desert? But, on the other hand, should not José have been happy to find such an easy prey?

Only the dog caused him some worry. He took the direction of the wind and described an arc around the camp so the dog would not catch his scent. For a long time he could see nothing but a tall silhouette standing in front of the fire, gesticulating. He continued to advance, taking care not to dislodge any stones. Eleazar was speaking passionately, his Bible in hand. His wife and children must have been seated in front of him, buried in their blankets. José crept so close to the minister that soon he could hear every word of his sermon.

The minister was speaking of the conversation he had had with the Indian chief. He had revealed to him his plan to settle in California. He had sketched out the simple life he intended to live there, based on the principles of the Bible.

"Brass Serpent listened to me carefully," he recounted. "He let me talk, and then he spoke in turn. He admitted to me the worries his people harbor against the invasion of the Pale Faces. He showed me his bow and his arrows, then he pointed to my old rifle.

" 'That is the difference between us,' he told me. 'For hunting, a bow is only effective from up to twenty yards away. The Indian hunter must get close to the buffalo herd and even mingle with it. He must adopt a special kind of dress, and modify his scent. He must employ the movements and gestures he learned as a boy from the master hunter. In truth, the Indian is the brother of the buffalo. He belongs to the same family as the wolf, the eagle, and the beaver. The buffalo gives the Indian his flesh to feed him, his skin to cover him, and his bones and his horns to make tools and weapons. The Indian loves and respects the buffalo in gratitude and filial piety. He accompanies him in all his migrations, and that is why we are here today.

" 'The man with the pale face is completely different. His rifle kills from three hundred yards. He is massacring the buffalo not out of necessity, but in order to trade his hide, and sometimes just for fun. Therefore we are seeing a frightening decrease in the number of buffalo. And with him, it is the survival of his brother the Indian that is threatened. The Pale Face does not belong to the great living family. He is the scourge of God!'

"These, my children, were the terrible words I heard from Brass Serpent. His look healed Benjamin. His mouth wounded me deeply. How could I answer him? I opened my Bible and chanced upon these lines that I read him: 'And the Lord God said, It is not good that the man should be alone; I will make him an help meet for him. And out of the ground the Lord God formed every beast of the field, and every fowl of the air; and brought them unto Adam to see what he would call them: and whatsoever Adam called every living creature, that was the name thereof. And Adam gave names to all cattle, and to the fowl of the air, and to every beast of the field; but for Adam there was not found an help meet for him' (Gen. 2.18–20).

"Thus the relationship between man and animal in Paradise was so close that God left it up to man to name each animal, and he even hoped that man would find an animal so similar to him that he could mate with it. But he was disappointed. And inspired by this disappointment he created woman to share man's bed.

"As for the animals, man's carnivorous diet forced him to kill them, whether they be wild or domesticated. And that is abominable. Indians lead a nomadic life, running from one end of the great prairie to the other, at the flanks of the buffalo herds. Their brothers the wolves do no differently.

"But we – emigrants from Ireland – we belong to the sedentary species, and, if we journey, it is only with the goal of finding a land to settle in. We know that this land is called California. There we will build our house, work our fields, and plant our orchards and our gardens. And we will answer to the vocation of sedentary peoples – farmers and plowmen – that is vegetarianism. We will eat only fruits and vegetables, never again shedding the blood of animals."

José had listened as in a dream to these words of peace and grandeur, and when Eleazar was silent, they were both looking down on the glowing logs that formed a cave full of sparks and crackling sounds. It seemed to José then that the voice of the minister had risen out of this fire, as the voice of Yahweh had emerged from the Burning Bush.

Suddenly he gave a start. Someone had just touched his hand.

Someone? No, not really, it was just a dog, and he recognized Blue, the husky with the light eyes that could see in the dark. The dog licked his hand, looking at him with his blue gaze. Instead of giving the stranger away by barking, he welcomed him as a friend, kissing his hand as dogs do, seemingly inviting him to come join the O'Braid family.

A little while later, when José decided to return to the camp of the Red Hand, he was not surprised to see that the dog was following him. His partners' stupor and admiration filled him with amused pride. They had been justifiably afraid of the animal. But there it was, tamed, harmless, even attentive at the heels of its new master!

Everyone found it quite natural that José would propose the next day to follow the O'Braid convoy and return to spy on it at night. So, as soon as night had fallen, he advanced toward the two wagons, which had progressed about twelve miles that day. The dog was still following him. When he stopped about thirty yards from the red glow of the fire he could see between the wagon wheels, the dog ran up to its masters, who welcomed it with shouts of joy. A distant and invisible observer of this affectionate reunion, José was touched in an inexplicable way. His emotion was even more powerful a few minutes later when, having inched a little closer, he witnessed this surprising nocturnal scene.

The fragile and venerable Irish harp had been taken out of the wagon and was resting between Esther's knees. Sitting on a sort of light wicker cathedra, she ran her fingers over the strings, leaning forward to discern the notes of the musical score propped up on a stand lit by the trembling light of two torches. The music floated on pure and plaintive waves toward a sky of jagged clouds illuminated by the full moon. It was truly the voice of the springs of green Ireland that rose out of the parched barrenness of the desert. And suddenly a hymn rang out, a chant of other voices, so different and so harmonious:

In our farmland the angels
Hover over our harvests.
In our villages the angels
Cover the roofs with their wings.
In our prairies the angels
Graze the grasses and the flowers.
Into our open hearts the angels
Carry gentleness and cheer.

A tide of emotion then swept over José when he heard the Latin hymn to the Virgin he used to sing with his little classmates, directed by the priest of the village!

Salve Regina, mater misericordiae,
Vita dulcedo et spes nostra, salve!

He found it hard to refrain from joining in song with the four Irish travelers! Later, the father, mother, and each one of the children took turns singing another song in a forceful, almost brutal rhythm:

ELEAZAR: I am the voice that cries out in the desert.

ESTHER: I am the sob that rolls down into the valley.

BENJAMIN: *I am the cry that rings out among the rocks.*

CORA: *I am the lament that drifts over the waves.*

ELEAZAR: *I am the clamor that salutes the coming of the Savior.*

ESTHER: *I am the confession that touches the heart of the Lord.*

BENJAMIN: *I am the laughter whose roar strikes the mountain.*

CORA: *I am the song that blooms on the lips of children.*

XVIII

Back in the Red Hand's camp, José noticed that this time the blue-eyed dog had not followed him.

The next morning, he revealed his plan to his cohorts. He was going to pretend to run into the O'Braids by chance, an emigrant traveling alone, going westward like them. In this way he would penetrate the Irish family and be well placed to disarm the minister when the Red Hand attacked. His partners' hearts were so hardened that none of them measured the cold shamelessness José would need to carry through this plan. They acquiesced, and it was agreed that they would meet one more time to finalize the last details.

The next day before noon, José, carrying a simple bundle of clothes over his shoulder, joined up with O'Braid and his family. It was easy, because the wagons were slowed down by the rugged ground, strewn with rocks and charred tree trunks. The minister feared nothing as much as serious damage to one of his wagons, and he was leading the horses with extreme caution. After introducing himself, José promptly offered to help Esther, who was driving the second wagon. He walked at the head of the horses, flanked by Benjamin and by Blue, who bounded with joy at his heels.

At nightfall, José accepted the family's offer to share their supper, but afterward he discreetly withdrew to unroll his blanket in the hollow of a rock, sheltered from the wind and out of sight of the others. He had perceived the nervous apprehension of the minister and wanted neither his behavior nor his words to upset him.

The next day, the dawn was still gray when Eleazar recited the morning prayer. Its purpose was always the same: to place the new day under the protection of God. Each of the four Irish folk pronounced in turn this magnificent exhortation of the mystic Angelus Choiselus: "Commence without fear and with a light heart the perilous voyage of life, love, and death. And do not worry: if you stumble, you will never fall lower than the hand of God!"

These words took on a different signification, depending on whether they came from the mouth of Eleazar, Esther, Benjamin, or Cora. Then all four, in one movement, turned their backs to the reddening sky to recommence their determined journey to the west. In the same way, each evening they faced the setting sun. Their shadows, which went before them in the morning, followed them in the evening. So they knew that they were proceeding in the right direction – toward the west, toward California.

As they advanced, the country was becoming drier and more arid. Soon they began seeing aloe, bristling with thorns, agave in the shape of candelabra, and prickly pears with their flat, hairy paddles. In the middle of the day, the heat became blistering. The minister reprimanded his children for drinking unnecessarily. Not only did the water have to be conserved, they would make themselves sick if they gave in too often to the irritation in their throat. They must not in any case exceed three quarts a day. It was a matter of will, and an excellent chance to exercise self control. They should be thinking about Jesus on the cross. He was thirsty, and the Roman soldiers gave him a vinegar-soaked sponge on the end of a pike.

The sun was beginning to sink toward the horizon when they made a macabre discovery. A corpse lay there on the sand, dressed in the outfit of a Mexican cowboy – a vaquero – wearing chaps and star shaped spurs. The dryness had reduced him to a hardened, leathery mummy, and apparently, neither four-footed nor winged scavengers had touched him.

His horse and his weapons must have been stolen. Eleazar leaned down toward his right hand and stood back up holding a crude piece of paper. With a bloody finger, the dying man had traced a few words in Spanish: "I had a friend. He robbed and killed me." The five travelers stood silent for a minute. Only José noticed the peculiar stare that Cora gave him. In spite of the heat, he broke out in a cold sweat. Then the minister opened his book of prayers and recited a funeral prayer for the stranger. But he decided then that they would continue on their way without burying the body.

During the night, José got up stealthily and walked in the direction where he knew he would find his accomplices of the Red Hand. They agreed that the attack would take place the day after next at midnight. Then José returned to the camp. He was a bit annoyed to see that once again Blue had followed him. It was absurd, of course, because a dog cannot speak. However, the memory of Cora's accusatory look continued to trouble him.

The next day, his decision was made. Besides, there was no

time to lose. He explained to the minister that, having discovered fresh tracks parallel to their own trail, he feared that bandits may be following. They must prepare for the worst. What weapons did the family have? The minister showed him his old rifle and a pistol. José set two revolvers before him. Tonight, he would give a shooting lesson to Benjamin. The young boy – barely recovered from his rattlesnake bite – looked at him excitedly. Esther too had to learn how to use a firearm, so the family would be defended by four guns. "And me? What will I do?" asked Cora. Her father put his arm around her: "Your transparent soul is the mirror of the world," he told her. "Whatever happens, you will be the inalterable witness of our fate."

A little while later, alone with José, she said to him:

"Blue told me everything. I know who you are!"

"Soon you will learn who I really am," José answered back. And he gave her a light caress on the cheek, as if to put her back in her role of the little girl.

She furrowed her brow angrily and turned her back on him.

The day after next, the night was dark and silent when José woke up Eleazar, Esther, and Benjamin. He thought he had heard the noise of stones underfoot, as if several men were coming, he explained. Unfortunately, he had not foreseen the minister's reaction when he revealed to him that the intentions of the strangers who were approaching could only be criminal, and that it was urgent that they shoot first.

"It's our only chance," he insisted.

"Shoot first at strangers we know nothing about?" the minister protested. "We would be the criminals!"

"Do you want to defend your children when they're dead?" José asked him desperately.

But he knew Eleazar well enough to understand that he would not give in. So he turned to Esther and Benjamin and positioned them under the first wagon with instructions to fire on anything they saw moving in the shadows. He then lay down on the canvas of the wagon so he could dominate the situation. The minister had taken his place on the second wagon with Cora.

José hoped to be the first to see the bandits, and the first to shoot. It was not to be. The first shot came from the side panels of the second wagon. A brief and confusing volley of shots followed. José shot in the direction of the flashes of gunfire he could make out in the dark. Then there was silence again, broken only by the sound, growing more and more faint, of one or two men running away over the rocky ground.

Immediately José jumped from his observation point and rejoined Esther and Benjamin. Both were safe and sound. They ran to the other wagon. It was from there that the first shot had rung out. José did not ask if it was the minister or Cora who had used the antiquated rifle. He was almost sure that it was Cora, but why fault the little girl, even if her actions had been decidedly excessive? The important thing was that she was not hurt. Unfortunately, the minister was not so lucky. He was lying motionless on his left side and showed José a wound bleeding from his right hip.

They noted too that one of the four horses – Coaly, the strongest, the most useful – had a fractured spine and would not be able to go on. Exploring the surroundings with a lantern, José discovered the bodies of two outlaws. He recognized Cunning Luis and One-Eyed Alejo. Lucky Felipe must have fled with Old Pedro. There wasn't much of a chance that they'd be back, but it would be a good idea to stay alert.

They tried to sleep a little, and at the first light of dawn they were bustling about the wagons. Esther treated the minister's wound. Alas, it was clear that he would not walk for a long time. José had to make up his mind to put down the black horse with a bullet to the ear, in spite of Cora's pleading. But it was out of the question that one of the wagons be pulled by a single horse. So they had to be content with one wagon and abandon the other with the furniture and objects they had decided to sacrifice. What tears and hesitations! But Esther did not have to say a word about saving the Irish harp. Everyone agreed to give it the place of honor in the wagon that would go on.

XIX

They started off again. José suggested they burn the wagon they were sacrificing with all its contents. The minister disagreed. Why deprive future emigrants of this unexpected inheritance?

He rode in the wagon by himself, next to the Irish harp. Benjamin led the way, riding Gus, his speckled roan. Esther walked with José beside the wagon pulled by Buck the colt and Grizzly the mare, Cora riding on her back. Esther's lameness – which she had tried to make everyone forget – would now be tested severely, alas. Nonetheless, everything would have been all right, if the minister had not suffered a thousand deaths as he was cruelly shaken about on the improvised mat they had arranged for him. He had no desire to eat and repeatedly asked for water, clearly exhausted by a high fever. Esther held his hand and spoke softly, trying to calm him.

The next day, the land began to rise: they had reached the first foothills of the Sierra Nevada. The heat broke and from time to time they would feel a cool breeze. Soon the travelers penetrated into a forest of pines and sequoias, bristling with rocks. They had to skirt a lake that was not on their map. They forded rushing streams with great difficulty, as the trail became increasingly steep. And they were guided by human graves, animal skeletons, ruins of old hearths, and the remains of broken wagons, grim warnings that they were on the right trail.

What would have become of them without José? Always cheerful, full of energy and ingenuity, he trapped rabbits, shot partridges, caught trout, and once even managed to kill a wild boar that furnished them with meat for several days.

As they climbed higher, the weather became brisk and the trail rougher. Sometimes they struggled mightily to get the wagon through a difficult passage. Would they be able to hold onto it until the end? No one spoke the question, but it was on all their minds. Soon the trees became sparse, and the night grew so cold that they had to keep the campfire burning till morning. The first patch of snow appeared when they had reached the summit of the pass, and it was a great joy for them.

But the next day they were struck by bad luck. When they emerged from their tents in the morning, they realized that the mare Grizzly had disappeared during the night. José studied her tracks to try to determine the direction she had taken. But to no avail. Perhaps she had simply turned back, obeying some obscure nostalgic instinct? After several hours of searching, helped by the dog Blue, they decided to leave without her. Two horses for one wagon: that was the minimum, but it could still work.

The higher altitudes, unfamiliar to them, held both good and bad surprises. One sunny afternoon the trail opened out onto a vast field of gentians: their mauve corollas seemed to go on forever, swaying in the breeze. Then there was a meadow thick with low bushes, laden with small purple berries. They were blueberries, and the family picked an ample supply, Eleazar recalling the manna that had miraculously fallen from heaven to feed the Hebrews as they crossed the Sinai desert. "California, California, blessed land, promised land!" he murmured in a kind of dream state. But his condition continued to worsen, for he barely ate at all.

One day they suffered through a storm of incredible fury and struggled to ford streams swelled by the torrential rains. They were soaked by the time night fell. They would have suffered bitterly from the cold had José not found a way to light a big fire in spite of the wet wood; they laughed and even Esther danced with the others around the fire, the vapor rising from their bodies, like horses after a race.

A last stroke of misfortune brought Esther to tears. A deep ravine cut across the trail. They laid tree trunks across it, which they hoped would hold the four wheels of the wagon they had emptied in order to lighten the load. One of the wheels slipped, and the vehicle tottered on the edge of the ravine. José slid underneath to examine the axles. When he came out, his face was pale and he was obviously reluctant to inflict the truth on his friends.

"The front axle is broken," he finally admitted.

"Which means?" asked Esther, already knowing the answer.

"Which means that we no longer have a wagon," declared José flatly.

The ensuing silence was unexpectedly broken by the minister.

"That's alright," he said, "I'll walk. Besides, I'm almost there. José, make me a walking stick."

Cora rushed into his arms, weeping.

"Papa, papa, why are you saying that you're almost there, when the road is still so long? I want to know. Answer me, papa!"

Eleazar looked down at the little girl, his eyes glassy, and then gently pushed her away. But everyone had noticed this mysterious utterance, and would remember it forever.

So they had to abandon the second wagon and secure to the horses' backs only the objects and sacks they valued most highly. Once again, they began by loading the harp, which they strapped onto Gus, Benjamin's speckled roan. As for the little bay, he would carry a few bags of clothes, the remaining flour and oats. The O'Braid family would most certainly be arriving in California like the poorest of the poor!

They pushed on, and everyone anxiously observed the uneven gait of the minister, leaning on the cane that José had fashioned for him. Silent, he gritted his teeth and stared straight ahead. During the halts, his lips moved in incoherent phrases, and given the solemn tone of his voice, they seemed to be quotations from Scripture.

The third day, the steep trail descended into a dense forest of cedars. The temperature warmed up considerably. Suddenly they came upon a vast clearing through which a sparkling stream flowed, and the five travelers stopped, overcome with joy.

Like a belvedere, the clearing provided a splendid view across the wide plain, green as far as the eye could see. It was an immense orchard of orange, lemon, and grapefruit trees, their fruits shining like dull gold in the shade of the leaves.

Esther and the children turned toward Eleazar. Tears flowed down his haggard face.

"California, land of milk and honey, so here you are, and your riches surpass the promises that God made to his wandering people," he declared weakly.

Then he asked José to approach, and he put his hand on his shoulder.

"The Spring and the Bush," he said in a stronger voice. "We must choose between this singing water that springs at our feet and descends into the valley, and the Burning Bush whose flame rises from the desert toward the heavens. Joshua, son of Nun, from the tribe of Ephraim, you will choose the spring. I entrust you with my people, Esther, Benjamin, and Cora, so that you may lead them safe and sound into the Promised Land. Be just and merciful."

"As for me, the Bush taught me that God would not permit me to descend into the living valley. No more than he would let Moses walk on the land of Canaan. Moreover, I have exhausted all my strength. I could not take another step. I can feel my life ebbing away. I order you to let me go alone to the place where God waits for me."

They obeyed his will, and he walked haltingly toward a small wood and disappeared. He stroked the leaves of a tree which he thought to be a sycamore, one last tender and discreet smile from his Irish land.

The next morning, Esther and the children went to pray over his body, and buried him in the light sand of the clearing he had chosen.

Later, José went back alone to this pure and primitive grave, and he meditated for a long time, conversing with the generous soul who had adopted him and given him new life.

Benjamin proudly took his place on the back of Gus, his little circus horse, and held in his arms the thirty stringed harp, as they descended among the flowers and fruits of the great California valley.